Mahabharata
and the
Marvellous
cycle of
Boons, Curses
and Vows

H.A. Padmini is a software professional dabbling with writing after her stint at Infosys. Born and brought up in Hyderabad, Padmini is an alumnus of Osmania University College of Engineering.

Keenly interested in writing since childhood, she has published quizzes, articles and stories. Padmini enjoys writing for children. A collection of her short stories for children titled *Tales of Anantha Bhargava Somayaji* has been recently published. This is her debut novel.

Padmini loves watching films, travelling and reading. Mythology and ancient lore are her passions. Currently she is reading up for her next book that is also based on mythology.

Padmini resides in Bangalore with her parents. She welcomes feedback and discussions on her work at hapadmini@hotmail.com

Mahabharata and the Marvellous Cycle of Boons, Curses and Vows

H.A. Padmini

Published by
Rupa Publications India Pvt. Ltd 2019
7/16, Ansari Road, Daryaganj
New Delhi 110002

Sales centres:
Allahabad Bengaluru Chennai
Hyderabad Jaipur Kathmandu
Kolkata Mumbai

Copyright © H.A. Padmini 2019

This book is based on the Mahabharata and its many versions. Many characters and incidents included here are fictional and part of the author's imagination. Any resemblance to any person, place or incident is purely coincidental. No offence is meant to any person, religion, caste, creed, ethnic group, etc. whatsoever. This story does not purport to be a complete narrative of all the events of the great Epic but is only a selective account of some portions of what is believed to have occurred in those days.

All rights reserved.

No part of this publication may be reproduced, transmitted, or stored in a retrieval system, in any form or by any means, electronic, mechanical, photocopying, recording or otherwise, without the prior permission of the publisher.

ISBN: 978-93-5333-547-2

First impression 2019

10 9 8 7 6 5 4 3 2 1

The moral right of the author has been asserted.

Printed by HT Media Ltd, Gr. Noida

This book is sold subject to the condition that it shall not, by way of trade or otherwise, be lent, resold, hired out, or otherwise circulated, without the publisher's prior consent, in any form of binding or cover other than that in which it is published.

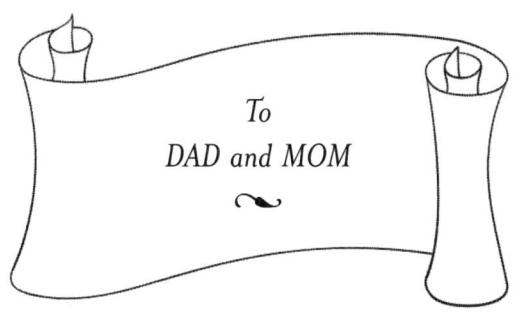

Contents

Prelude ix

Part I: The Beginning
1. Birth of Sage Vedavyasa 3
2. Descent of Devi Gangaa 8
3. The Eighth Vasu—Devavrata 23
4. Satyavati's Progeny—Chitrangada and Vichitraveerya 30
5. A Clash of Vows 34
6. A Vow of Vengeance and a Boon 40
7. Sage Vedavyasa Sires the Bharata Clan 44
8. Sahasrakavaci, the Mighty Demon King 51
9. Durvasa's Boon: The Story of Kunti 57
10. Karna: A Boon-child Is Cursed 62

Part II: Narayana–The Upholder of Dharma
1. Kamsa's Story 71
2. The Chosen Couple—Devaki and Vasudeva 75
3. Yashoda and Krishna 80
4. Salvation for Demons and Demonesses 84
5. Kamsa Meets His End 89

Part III: The Stage Is Set

1. Yudhisthira—Dharma on Earth ... 93
2. Bhima, the Brother of Hanuman ... 101
3. Arjuna—Nara Reborn ... 105
4. The Ashwini Twins ... 110
5. Pandu's Story ... 119
6. Gandhari's Story ... 124
7. The Transformation of Shikhandi ... 129
8. Nalayani's Five Boons and Draupadi ... 133

Part IV: The Great Churning

1. Drona and Drupada ... 139
2. Karna and Duryodhana: an Unlikely Friendship ... 144
3. Hastinapur ... 147
4. Duryodhana's Treachery ... 161
5. The Exile ... 163

Part V: The Great War

1. Bhisma's Leadership ... 181
2. Drona Meets His End ... 188
3. Curses Come Together for Karna ... 193
4. Beginning of the Inevitable ... 197
5. Duryodhana's End ... 199
6. After the War ... 204
7. The End of Dwapara Yuga ... 206

Epilogue ... 213
Acknowledgements ... 217

Prelude

We are living in the Kali Yuga. This is said to be the fourth and final *yuga* after which the entire world will come to an end and submerge in God. A new world will then be created (*kalpaksaye praliiyante kalpaadau visrjaamyaham:* At the end of the *kalpa*, i.e. a cycle of four yugas, all creations are withdrawn and at the beginning of another kalpa, are released again), so say our elders. The Puranas, which give the concept of relative time, say that one day of Brahma, the creator, is called 'kalpa', and one kalpa comprises four yugas.

The previous three yugas were Satya or Krita Yuga, Treta Yuga, and Dwapara Yuga. A complete kalpa cycle starts with a Golden Age, called the Satya or Krita Yuga and ends in the Dark Age, or Kali Yuga. The consecutive yugas see a gradual decline of Dharma—virtue, wisdom, knowledge, intellectual capability, lifespan, and emotional and physical strength. This is beautifully depicted with the metaphor of an animal. It is said that in Satya/Krita Yuga, Dharma is represented as an animal with all its four feet firmly implanted on the earth. The four feet of Dharma are *tapas* 'penance', *shaucam* 'purity', *dayaa* 'compassion', and *satya* 'truth'. This implies that Dharma was firmly practised during the Satya Yuga. By the end of the Treta Yuga, Dharma stands on two legs. At the end of Dwapara Yuga, Dharma is said to be standing on only one leg. Finally, in the Kali Yuga, Dharma is completely lost when it raises all its four feet and flies away.

Dharma is said to be the foundation of the entire world (*dharmo vishvasya jagatah pratisthaa*), at the loss of which, the foundation of life is utterly weakened. And the world hurtles towards inevitable dissolution.

The Ramayana and the Mahabharata, the two great epics of the Treta and Dwapara yugas respectively, are the perennial rivers that have inundated the vast land of legendary Indian culture, mythology, tradition, and ethos for the past countless centuries. The Ramayana and Mahabharata instruct us in the four goals of life (*purusaarthas*): *dharma* 'virtue', *artha* 'wealth', *kaama* 'enjoyment', and *moksa* 'salvation', and include all that happened in earlier times (*dharmaarthakaamamoksaanaam upadeshasamanvitam/ puurvavrttam kathaayuktam itihaasam pracaksyate*).

It is said that the Mahabharata was dictated by Vedavyasa and was written by Lord Ganesha. When Vedavyasa approached Ganesha to act as scribe, he agreed at once but put a condition that he should not have to pause any time. So whenever Vedavyasa had to pause and think awhile, or gather his thoughts, he would come up with a 'twister' which Ganesha had to unravel before writing it. Vedavyasa first narrated the Mahabharata to his son Shuka. Later he expounded it to other disciples. It is believed that Narada related the Mahabharata to the *Devas* or gods while Shuka taught it to the *Gandharvas, Rakshasas* and *Yakshas*. One of Vedavyasa's favourite disciples Vaisampayana revealed the epic for the benefit of humanity when Janamejaya, son of King Parikshit, conducted a great *yagna*. Afterwards, this great story was recited by *Suuta*, a 'traditional narrator' in the forest of Naimisha to the assembly of sages lead by Sage Shaunaka.

The Kali Yuga has begun a long time ago but we have no epic—only stories and narratives to describe the various historical personages and incidents. So in the Yuga of Kali we continue to use the Ramayana and the Mahabharata as beacons. The Mahabharata is a microcosm of our lives in the true sense, and its teachings are relevant for the modern age as well.

The Mahabharata is the story of how one should lead one's life, how one's deeds affect one's life, and how these are carried over into one's next life. Each person carries a ledger of actions—right and wrong—in which entries are made and a Balance Sheet of sorts is drawn at one's death that determines the path a soul will take in its next birth.

By reading about the previous lives and the next births, one is able to see the thread of continuity. The essence of our lives is in this great cycle of *Karma*—everything is connected in a cosmic pattern, though we focus only on the life we are currently living. The answers to many questions, to things that seem inexplicable in this life, are in these interconnections—and this is one of the great lessons the Mahabharata teaches us.

The Mahabharata is the saga of innumerable characters who will remain with us forever and guide us in our attempt to understand various incidents and situations in our lives, and show us how to work towards salvation.

Let us use the Mahabharata to light our way!

Part I

The Beginning

chapter 1

Birth of Sage Vedavyasa

King Viswamitra was on a hunting expedition with a large convoy of courtiers and soldiers when he chanced upon the hermitage of Sage Vasistha on the summit Gurushikhara, a part of the Aravalli range. As was the custom, the sage welcomed the king and spread out a lavish feast in his honour. After everyone was fed and rested, King Viswamitra asked Vasistha how it was possible for an ascetic to feed such a huge retinue without any prior arrangement or notice. And in such a short time, too!

Sage Vasistha smiled, 'O mighty King, I am blessed with Nandini, the daughter of the heavenly cow Kamadhenu, who resides in my household. There is nothing in this world that Nandini cannot grant. It is because of her bountiful gifts that I can perform sacrifices and please the Gods. I need nothing else since Nandini fulfils all my wishes.'

On hearing this, the king was seized with the desire to possess Nandini. 'Such a divine creature should grace the king's palace, not the hut of a sage', he said. 'You should gift me Nandini since I am your king, and I am asking this of you. You can take what you will in exchange; I open my treasury to you.'

But the sage would have nothing of this. 'What would I do with wealth, my lord, I who am an ascetic? It is enough that I have Nandini—I cannot give her away.' But King Vishwamitra would brook no refusal. When Vasistha refused to part with Nandini despite his many requests, offers, and finally command, the king tried to take Nandini by force but failed. Later, the king gained special powers through austerities and Vishwamitra caused the hundred sons of Sage Vasistha to be devoured by a demon!

A sage's wrath is the most terrible thing, and the king had invited it! When Vasistha came to know of this, he was heartbroken. He summoned all his great powers and quelled the anger that was about to well up inside him—he was a *Brahmarshi* after all! With tremendous self-control the sage stopped himself from uttering a curse that would have instantly and completely ruined the king and his kingdom. But the father in him was overcome with grief—his hundred sons, what had they done to deserve this? How could he bear this loss? What a terrible waste of lives—and all because of him! Thoughts of giving up his life filled Vasistha, but knowing suicide is a sin, he quelled those thoughts as well and returned home.

As he entered the hermitage he heard the chanting of Vedic verses. Adrisyanti, his eldest son Shakti's wife, was pregnant, and the child within her was reciting the Vedas! This child, born posthumously, was named Parashara. Parashara grew up to be an expert in astrology and a famous law-giver like Manu. Parashara eventually became one of the *gotra pravartakas* or sages from whom the *gotras* or patriarchal lineages originate.

On one of his travels, young Parashara halted on the banks of the river Yamuna, in the house of a fisherman chieftain. When dawn broke, the fisherman asked his daughter Matsyagandhi, (meaning, One with the smell of fish)—who had, as an infant, been found by a fisherman in the stomach of a fish—to row the sage across the river. Matsyagandhi was beautiful and at the peak of her youth. Immune to her physical attraction, and deep in a meditative trance, Parashara sat in the boat as she began to row him across. After a few minutes, a voice seemed to speak to him from the skies. It said 'Parashara, be aware of your surroundings. The time is very auspicious and whatever you do now will yield fruit beneficial to mankind. It is most opportune to father a son.'

Parashara opened his eyes and saw Matsyagandhi who was busy rowing. He realized both of them were together, isolated from the rest, and he had to seize the moment. Parashara expressed his desire but the maiden was too shy to accept him. So Parashara created a dense mist all around the boat, making it invisible from any human eye, and convinced her to accept him. Realizing she was with no ordinary man, Matsyagandhi acquiesced and Parashara created an island out of his spiritual power. The mist covered the two of them from the prying eyes of the world. Parashara looked at her from head to foot and his eyes shone with a divine light. The light bathed Matsyagandhi in a golden hue and she gave birth to a son.

She fell at his feet. 'O Sage! Why have you done this to me? I am unmarried. Who will marry me now? What shall I do with this newborn baby? How can I rear him?' Parashara soothingly replied, 'Do not weep. This son of yours will render great service to mankind and his name will live forever. I will take him with me and be responsible for his upbringing. You need not worry on that count. Regarding your being unmarried, I will restore you to your original self with my powers and I shall also grant you a boon as well. Ask what you desire.'

Matsyagandi quickly gathered her wits and asked that the foul smell that pervaded her body be removed forever. Parashara granted her the boon and named her Yojanagandhi or one whose fragrance spreads across a *yojana*, a measurement of distance akin to four kilometres. Parashara then sprinkled some holy water on the newborn baby. The child grew into a man immediately and bowed to his parents. He was named Krishna Dwaipayan, the dark one born on an island—'Krishna' meaning dark and 'Dwipa' meaning island.

He addressed his mother thus: 'I am indebted to you for having brought me to this world. I shall go for penance. Whenever you need my help, you just have to remember me and call out my name thrice. I shall appear at your service.' So saying, he vanished. Yojanagandhi resumed rowing the boat and after Parashara alighted on the banks, she returned to her home. She eventually came to be known as Satyavati.

Krishna Dwaipayan grew up to become famous as Sage Vedavyasa since he was responsible for the division of the great Vedic lore into four groups—Rig, Yajur, Saama, and Atharva—for the use of the four officiating priests in a yagna. Vedavyasa was an incarnation of Lord Vishnu (*vyaasaaya vishnuruupaaya vyaasaruupaaya vishnave*: to Vyasa who is a form of Vishnu and Vishnu who is a form of Vyasa).

Sage Vedavyasa would in future sire, by Vichitraveeraya's wives, the fathers of both the Kauravas and the Pandavas who fought the war of Mahabharata—a war to establish Dharma or the victory of good over evil. He would also have a son of his own, Shuka, who later became a great *gyaani* as well as a devotee of Narayana from his very birth.

It is Shuka who narrates the Bhagavata, comprising the many tales of Narayana and his several incarnations, dwelling in detail on the exploits of Narayana as Sri Krishna, to Parikshit, the grand-son of Arjuna. There is a famous verse which gives the lineage of Vyasa thus: *vyaasam vasisthanaptaaram shakteh pautram akalmasam/ paraasharaatmajam vande shukataatam taponidhim:* I bow to Vyasa, great-grandson of Vasistha, grandson of Shakti, son of Parashara, father of Shuka, and himself a great saint.

chapter 2

Descent of Devi Gangaa

King Shantanu was a ruler of the Kuru dynasty, and his capital was Hastinapur. He was valorous and ruled his kingdom righteously. In the Treta Yuga, Shantanu had been born as Mahabhisha in the Ikshvaku dynasty. Mahabhisha was a valiant king and had attained the ability to move about in heaven (*Swarga*). One day, Mahabhisha was in discussion with Brahma and other gods. While they were talking on various aspects of life, Gangaa came to meet Brahma. As soon as she entered all eyes turned towards her and drank in her beauty. Her limbs were perfect, her waist thin, her breasts voluptuous and her hips moved like the waves on a seashore. She had come to meet her father, Brahma, to take his leave to visit her friends. Seeing her, Vaayu, the god of wind, was so enamoured of her beauty that he could not control himself and sighed deeply. Immediately her thin veil flew up in the wind. Though all eyes were fixed on her until then, that very instant all present lowered their eyes out of respect for Gangaa. But Mahabhisha, transfixed by her loveliness, continued to stare at her. He could not take his eyes off her, such was her beauty. Seeing such indiscretion, Brahma called out, 'Ye Mahabhisha! How dare you indulge in such lewd behaviour? Lower your eyes!' But even so, Mahabhisha could not control himself and continued to shamelessly ogle at Gangaa. Brahma was enraged at this. His eyes reddened and trembling with anger he cursed Mahabhisha thus: 'You are besotted by Gangaa's physical form. May the same cause you incalculable grief! You have lost your right to be in heaven. You will be born on earth and suffer out this curse. Since you have desired her you shall have her, but she will bring you sorrow immeasurable!'

And so was Mahabhisha cursed to be born on earth with Gangaa as his wife—a wife who would do unkind deeds unto him, thereby making him miserable.

Because of his countless noble deeds, Mahabhisha was born as Shantanu and ruled Hastinapur wisely. One day when he was passing by a river on his stallion, he decided to spend some time on the riverbank, enjoying pristine nature. He got off from his horse and went towards the river. There he saw a beautiful lady sitting on a boulder and looking at the sunset. King Shantanu was stunned by her exquisite features and fine-looking skin. She was doe-eyed, slender, with luscious lips and a small waist. He approached her without making a sound but when he neared her and wanted to surprise her, she turned by herself and looked at him questioningly.

'I am King Shantanu, the ruler of Hastinapur. Fair lady, tell me who you are. Why are you alone here? It is not safe for such a beautiful woman to wander alone.' He spoke with concern. The maiden, who was Goddess Gangaa in human form, replied, 'There is no fear for people who are ruled by a king like you. In your kingdom a gorgeous woman decked in jewels may roam unhurt even in the dead of night.' King Shantanu was pleased with her answer and felt encouraged. He slowly moved nearer to her. He took her hand in his own and said, 'O Beautiful One! I am mesmerized by your lovely self. I wish to make you mine. Will you marry me?' Without realizing, King Shantanu was holding Gangaa's hand in his. Gangaa delicately retrieved her hand and smilingly responded, 'I am honoured by your proposal. I would be happy to be your wife. However, you must accept some conditions of mine before I marry you.'

'I am ready to do whatever you ask of me', declared the besotted Shantanu. 'Please give due thought before you agree to my stipulations, for they may not be easy to follow—even for a king. You or anyone else must never ask me who I am or where I come from. You must never question me or my actions. You must not stop me from doing anything that I want to—whether you understand the reason for it or not. You must not say anything to displease me. The moment you do any of these, I will leave you forever. If you break your word nothing can change my decision to leave you that very moment.' She said all this with a winning smile that went straight to Shantanu's heart. Shantanu was rather relieved that there were no difficult deeds to be done to win her hand. Listening to her golden voice he felt that her restrictions were not out of the ordinary; quite simple in fact. He accepted her conditions swiftly saying, 'I do not believe that one like you will ever do anything wrong or untrustworthy. I have full faith in you and promise to never question you. Do not worry. There will never be a situation wherein you can even think of leaving me. I will be with you till my last breath. I will order everyone in the kingdom to behave in accordance with your wishes.'

King Shantanu brought the lovely lady to his palace and their marriage was performed with due grandeur and splendour. They loved each other and lived in bliss. Soon Gangaa was pregnant with King Shantanu's child. In the seventh month all traditional rites were suitably performed in the palace itself as Gangaa had claimed that she had no parental home to retire to, nor had any family. The coming of the child was awaited with much eagerness by all. A son was born and the entire kingdom rejoiced hearing the news. Shantanu's happiness knew no bounds and he thanked god for having blessed him with such a wife and son.

That night King Shantanu was woken by the rustle of clothes and the wails of his son. He saw his wife leave the room with their son. He got out of bed and followed her finding her movements suspicious. She slowly moved along the corridors and reached the terrace of the palace. King Shantanu followed her at a distance wondering why she was roaming around in the night but remembering that he could not ask her any question, kept silent. She went near the edge of the terrace that overlooked the river. In one swift movement she flung the baby swathed in cloth into the river! King Shantanu was so shocked that no sound came out even though his mouth had opened to scream in anger. But it remained a silent scream as he remembered the vow he had made to Gangaa. Horrified and beside himself with the cruelty of the woman he so dearly loved, Shantanu returned to the chamber, moving swiftly to reach before Gangaa returned. He lay in bed and pretended to be asleep. After a few minutes, Gangaa came in and lay down beside him without a word. As soon as she fell asleep Shantanu left the room and wept like a child. The disappearance of the infant prince was spoken about in the entire kingdom but in whispers. No one dared to bring their doubts into the open as King Shantanu's orders carried a death penalty if broken.

A few months later Gangaa became pregnant again. This time king Shantanu felt no delight; he was plagued by what he had seen happen to his first son. Again Gangaa drowned the baby as soon as it was born. King Shantanu continued to remain silent though he found it difficult to internalize his grief. He maintained his composure in his wife's presence but would break down in solitude. Gangaa seemed indifferent; the king's tear-stained face was obvious to everyone but she made no reference to it. In this manner Gangaa threw seven of their offsprings into the river.

In due course Gangaa was expecting for the eighth time. This time King Shantanu decided that he would not tolerate

Gangaa's actions anymore and would try to save his son. He was on his guard. He felt that she had misused his integrity, so would never leave him if she was stopped from killing their offspring. He could not imagine that any woman would leave her husband just because he stopped her from murdering her own child. He spent all his time with her fearing that she may not wait until the birth of the child to kill it. King Shantanu had become paranoid.

The time for delivery had come. The court physician came accompanied by the midwife and after an examination told the King that his child would soon be entering this world. King Shantanu paced in front of the room and was soon rewarded with the happy news—'O Mighty King! A son has been born to continue your line. May you be pleased to welcome him into this world', said the midwife. King Shantanu rewarded her with a gold neckpiece and hastened to the bedside of Gangaa. A tiny baby boy lay by her side. Shantanu was thrilled. He stretched out his hands to take the child into his arms. Gangaa, who was reposing, got up suddenly, and clasping the infant to her breast, hurried out. King Shantanu followed her hurrying figure praying that he would be able to reach her in time to save his son. Gangaa headed for the terrace overlooking the river to throw the baby. It was the same place from where she had killed their seven sons born earlier. She raised her arms but before she could throw the baby into the waters, King Shantanu leapt to her side and snatched the baby from her hands. He raged, 'What kind of a mother are you, you heartless woman! You have killed all my sons. I will not allow you to murder again. Why are you behaving in this manner? What sins have these newborn babies committed that you are consigning them into the swirling waters? I will not allow you to kill any more of my children. I should have done this much before and saved all my children. Answer me. Why have you behaved thus?'

Gangaa smiled and without answering any of his questions said, 'My dear husband, you had promised never to question me or my actions. Now that you have done so, I can no longer live with you.' King Shantanu was startled at her words. He had not expected that she would stick to what she had said when he had proposed marriage to her. He began pleading with her but she remained adamant. She said, 'I have to leave you. I will not kill your son but will bring him up and educate him suitably. When he comes of age, I will return him to you.'

When King Shantanu realized that she would not relent he tried reasoning with her. He said, 'I do not understand your actions. Pray at least tell me why you have been committing the sin of killing your own sons. The almighty god will never forgive you. How can you remain so calm and composed?'

Gangaa gave a long sigh. 'What you have witnessed is the ending of a curse that was pronounced ages ago, dear husband. I owe it to you to tell you what had happened in earlier lives.' And she related to him the story of Mahabhisha.

When she ended, Shantanu was overcome by grief. 'Ah!' he said, 'Now I realize why you agreed to become my wife so easily. I will now have to suffer for the rest of my life as my life will be a barren desert without you. But dearest, I cannot understand why *you* had been punished in this fashion. Why have you been made to commit the terrible cruelty to these children of ours. What had *they* done in their previous lives to be killed in this fashion?'

'There is so much more to tell you, dear husband', Gangaa said. 'So many lives are interconnected by so many deeds, boons and curses!' And she began to narrate the story of her earlier birth.

༺

Vasus and the curse of Vasistha

The Vasus are a class of eight deities—Dhara, Anala, Ap, Anila, Dhruva, Soma, Pratyuusa and Prabhasa. They were Indra's attendants, and are counted among the thirty-three gods, along with the twelve Adityas—Mitra, Varuna, Aryaman, Daksha, Bhaga, Amsha, Tvashta, Savitaa, Pooshan, Shakra, Vivaswat and Vishnu; the eleven Rudras—Ajaikapaat, Ahirbudhnya, Pinaaki, Aparaajita, Rta, Pitruruupa, Triambaka, Vrushaakapi, Shambhu, Havana, Eshwara; and the Ashwini twins—Dasra and Nasatya.

The eight brothers were together called the Vasus, children of Dharma's wife, Vasu. Vasu was one of Prajapati Daksha's daughters. One day the eight Vasus went to Sage Vasistha's hut on Mount Meru, accompanied by their wives.

They were given a warm welcome and served with food deserving of a king. They were very pleased with the courtesy shown to them. After they had rested, the wife of Prabhasa, the youngest Vasu, said to her husband, 'I wonder how this sage served us such excellent food at such short notice. His hermitage does not seem to hold enough to provide for such a feast. It appears magical. Please ask him the secret of this. I am sure there is something behind it all, for how else is it possible to provide such royal comforts in this remote and inaccessible place?' Curiosity got the better of all, and since they could not find any plausible explanation, they decided to ask their host Sage Vasistha.

They approached Sage Vasistha and spoke with reverence, 'Holy Sir, we are very happy with the food and comforts that you provided us. But we cannot understand how such hospitality is possible for you. Pray, tell us the secret.' Sage Vasistha smiled and led them to the back of the hut where there was a cowshed. There stood a magnificent cow the like of which even the Vasus had never seen! It was pure milky white and had large beatific eyes. Her udder was full and her calf was playing with her tail. Sage Vasistha bowed to the cow and turning to the Vasus said, 'Behold Nandini, the daughter of Kamadhenu, the holy cow, the great provider who fulfils every desire and want. She is more than a wishing tree. I serve her and she takes care of all my needs.'

The sight of Nandini provoked similar feelings in the Vasus as it had done in King Vishwamitra. They were filled with greed and the youngest, Prabhasa, also called Dyasu, egged by his wife, voiced his feelings openly, 'Holy Sir, why do you need such a cow? It is of no use to hermits. Give it to us so that we may enjoy all the pleasures of the world. We would like to own it.' The other Vasus supported him and did not dissuade him when he untied Nandini and began to lead her away.

Sage Vasistha was very angry at this open greed and ill-mannered act, especially after he had lavished care on all the Vasus and their wives. So enraged was he at their betrayal of his hospitality, that he cursed them loud and clear: 'This cow is holy to me and to the entire world. She has been given to me by Indra so that I can perform sacrificial rites using her help. She provides me everything I need to conduct the rites and rituals for the welfare of the whole world. How dare you try to steal her? You yourselves are considered to be gods and yet have debased yourselves with greed, behaving like common thieves. I curse you to be born as humans on the earth and endure a life of suffering and attachment, and understand what it is to be a mortal!'

As soon as the curse was uttered, the Vasus were struck with terror and mortification. Immediately, the eight Vasus realized their mistake and fell at Sage Vasistha's feet. 'Forgive us, O Reverend Sage! We have committed an unpardonable sin. But we beg of you, show us mercy and retract your curse.' The moment of anger having passed, Sage Vasistha had calmed down as is usual with great men. Their hearts will be harder than diamond, and softer than flowers when the situation demands: *vajraadapi kathoraani mrduuni kusumaadapi*. Seeing their tear-streaked repentant faces, he felt that he had been too harsh on them. However, there was no way even he could take back a curse once uttered—so potent and powerful is a curse uttered by a sage.

Vasistha said, 'A curse once uttered is like an arrow that has been released from a bow. Though I am a Brahmarshi and have full control over my sense organs, I was angered and a curse escaped my lips. This can only mean one thing—that the curse is for your own good and for the good of the world. You need to know that as Vasus you should be exemplary in your behaviour. Any mistake on your part will have huge repercussions. However, since you have realized your fault quickly I shall modify my curse so that you are redeemed quickly—your mortal life will be very short. Find a mother who will kill you as soon as you are born, and you can return immediately to heaven. But the youngest of Vasus, Prabhasa, who was the chief perpetrator of the crime, must, however, live out his life as a human being on earth. There is no respite for him. He committed this crime because of his wife. Therefore he shall be deprived of conjugal bliss. And he shall meet his end because of a woman. He shall not get married or bear children and thus will not become bound by the wheel of karma, and return to heaven on his death. But he will be an illustrious man and become famous for his vow of celibacy. So the curse has been softened with boons. All of you may leave now.'

The Vasus implored in one voice, 'O Great Sage! You have been kind to us by lessening the time of our mortal existence and allowing us to return to our heavenly abode almost instantly. But pray who will be our parents? And how can we find a woman who will agree to kill her seven children at birth? This is an impossible solution. Kindly guide us.'

Sage Vasistha shut his piercing eyes for a moment. 'Seek Gangaa and she will help you.'

As instructed by Sage Vasistha, the eight crest-fallen Vasus approached Gangaa diffidently. 'O Mother Gangaa, please bless us. We need your help'.

'What is it, my sons?'

'Mother, you have addressed us as your sons. Please give us your word that you will grant us our only wish, and we ask no more. Only then will we be able to open our hearts to you', Prabhasa said.

They related what had happened to them at Vasistha's hermitage and their plight. They requested for the boon that they would be born to Gangaa and that she would drown them immediately after their birth—to live out Sage Vasistha's curse. Gangaa was only the means to an end, doing as was ordained.

⁓

King Shantanu was listening to Gangaa, overwhelmed by what he had just heard. His sons were none other than the eight Vasus! And his wife was none other than the celestial Gangaa in human form!

Then a thought struck him. The Vasus were living out a curse and so was he. But why was Gangaa made to come down to earth as a human being? The king turned to Gangaa and held her hand in his. 'Dearest, tell me why were you chosen to suffer in this mortal world? What sin had you committed? Though I have never loved anyone or anything as much as I have loved you, tell me, have you never loved me at all? Has our conjugal life been just a chore you had to fulfil? Won't you feel any agony when you leave me?'

Gangaa looked at the king with sympathy and said, 'One has to bow before destiny, dear husband... Therefore I took the form of a beautiful woman and, biding my time, met you and as promised, helped in the release of the Vasus from their mortal birth, ensured the fulfillment of your curse, and liberated myself from mine, too.

'I understood that there was a special reason why the Vasus had been asked to come to me, though they themselves did not know about it. I had to bear this because of what had happened aeons ago, when I was young and careless!'

So saying, Gangaa proceeded to tell him of another birth and another curse.

Gangaa's story: the unravelling

'Lord Vishnu in his Vamana avatar of a boy ascetic approached King Bali and asked the king for land that he could cover in three paces. King Bali granted him his wish. Immediately Vishnu assumed gigantic proportions and covered the earth with one foot and the heavens with the other. Realizing who the boy really was, King Bali requested Vishnu to place his foot on his head in order to complete the third step. Vishnu did so and King Bali was thus pushed into the underworld. At this time Brahma washed Vishnu's feet with water from his *kamandalu* (water-pot) and from this water, I was born. I was then given to Himavan and his wife Menaka to be their first daughter, and a sister to Parvati.

During those days there was a mighty and fearsome sage, Sage Durvasa. During one of his visits to heaven, a gust of wind had blown away the single piece of cloth that covered him and I, foolish and innocent as I was, had laughed at the sight of his nakedness. Sage Durvasa was enraged and as was his wont, cursed me to be born as a mortal. So, when the Vasus came to me with the request to be their mortal mother, I knew my time to fulfil Sage Durvasa's curse had come.'

Slowly withdrawing her hand from Shantanu's, Gangaa sighed softly. 'Dear husband, I have to leave you now. But await the return of your eighth born whom I am taking away with me. I shall bring your grownup son to you who will not be an ordinary man, as you now know.' So saying, Gangaa disappeared with their son in her arms.

King Shantanu was inconsolable with the loss of his beloved queen and sons. He turned to a life of solitude and prayer, ruling wisely and righteously, conscious of how each heedless action can affect the future.

So are all of us parts of a great wheel of destiny, drawn together and leading our lives as decreed by boons and curses and actions of past-lives. The Vasus came to be born of Gangaa, so that they could redeem their curse of being mortal for one day, and return to heaven once again. Ganga had to come down to earth as a woman to redeem Durvasa's curse that she be born as a mortal and live on earth. King Shantanu had to suffer the grief of losing seven sons and also his wife because he had been cursed by Brahma in his previous life as Mahabhisha.

Thus it was the fulfillment of individual curses and boons coming together, that led all of them to come together in one lifecycle. The wheel of destiny is thus affected by our own deeds, and what we do in one life influences the path taken in another birth.

chapter 3

The Eighth Vasu—Devavrata

King Shantanu spent several years as a celibate. He would spend almost every evening near the river hoping that Gangaa would see his sorrow and return to him. When Gangaa had left with his eighth son, King Shantanu could not do anything to stop her because he was bound by his word. Also the knowledge of what had happened in earlier lifetimes had shaken him. However, he still hoped that Gangaa would return to him someday. It was this vain hope that stopped him from desiring other women. Many years passed in this way. One day, as was his wont, King Shantanu went to the riverbank in the evening. There he saw a boy in his teens playing with his bow and arrows. As King Shantanu watched, the boy created a structure with his arrows that stopped the flow of the river. The king was struck with wonder at the boy's skill. He approached him and said, 'I am pleased with your proficiency in archery. Whose son are you?' The boy saluted him and replied, 'I am Devavrata, the son of Gangaa.'

King Shantanu was amazed! Barely concealing his elation he quickly asked, 'Where is your mother? I want to see her. Can you take me to her?' The boy called out to his mother, who appeared in all her glory. She looked fondly at her son and at the king. Then she addressed the king thus: 'O King, I am here to present you this boy who is your son. I have cared for and brought him up with much love and attention. I have named him Devavrata. He will also be known as Gaangeya—the son of Gangaa. He has been educated by Shukracharya, the guru of the asuras; Brihaspati, the guru of the gods; and by Parashurama, feared by all the Kshatriyas. He is a competent warrior like a true Kshatriya. I have made him worthy of being called your son. Take him with you, O King. My duty here is over. I must now return to my abode.' So saying, Gangaa approached her son and embracing him lovingly led him to King Shantanu. Devavrata touched King Shantanu's feet and the father raised the son up by his shoulders and encircled him in his arms. In this emotional moment between father and son, Gangaa disappeared, returning to her celestial abode.

Shantanu took his son Devavrata to the palace.

Shantanu was ecstatic to get back his son whom he had missed all these years. His dreary loneliness was now filled with familial bliss. King Shantanu tried to find out everything about his son—his childhood spent with his mother Gangaa, his training under the three greatest of gurus—Shukracharya, Brihaspati and Parashurama; his interests, habits, likes and dislikes. As days passed, King Shantanu discovered to his joy that his son was the epitome of courage and valour. Now a happy man, King Shantanu spent most of his time with his son, teaching him the intricacies of statecraft, preparing him to rule the kingdom which would one day be naturally his.

Since Devavrata had studied scriptures under the guidance of Brihaspati, the preceptor of the gods, and history, geography, science and administration under Shukracharya, he was extremely well informed. At a young age he had crystal clear thoughts on issues like politics, welfare of citizens, agriculture, taxation, philosophy, spirituality and law. His teacher Parashurama had made him the best in the art of weaponry. None could defeat Devavrata in strategy or battle. He was the best archer and swordsman in the entire kingdom and his name soon spread to all surrounding kingdoms.

Devavrata was completely devoted to his father and to the service of the kingdom. He became the darling of the masses in no time and people eagerly awaited his coronation. Though he was very happy with his father, Devavrata missed his mother. He would, therefore, frequently go to the river bank and speak with her. He asked her to come and stay with them in the palace but she refused. She never explained the reason though.

Years passed and soon Devavrata grew into a handsome man, loved and cherished by one and all. King Shantanu ruled the kingdom in name but all his duties were excellently taken care of by prince Devavrata. Once it so happened that King Shantanu wished to discuss the taxes levied on the fisherfolk of his kingdom who lived by the riverside. He wanted to meet the leader of the fishermen, so he decided to pay a visit to the chieftain's house. But the chieftain was away and his daughter was in the hut. This daughter was none other than Matsyagandhi who had been given the boon of fragrance by Parashara Muni, and was now called Yojanagandhi and Satyavati. As soon as King Shantanu entered the chieftain's hut a divine fragrance charmed his nostrils. He was still reeling under its effect when he was received by a young lissome girl who led him to a mat. She seated him and took her place in front of him. King Shantanu's breath was taken away by her beauty. Her aura was so intoxicating that King Shantanu could not desist and proposed marriage to her immediately. Satyavati, delighted though she was at being wooed by the king, was a dutiful daughter and demurely answered him thus: 'O King, I am honoured by your proposal. But I cannot accept it or answer you in any way. You must approach my father first. I will obey his wish.'

King Shantanu was so bewitched that he decided to await the chieftain's homecoming instead of returning to the palace. The chieftain returned the next morning with his haul of fish and was surprised to find the king sitting in his humble abode. Seeing him, King Shantanu, instead of discussing taxes as was the need, directly asked for Satyavati's hand. The poor fisherman could not believe his ears. But he was a wily one and he thought about it for a while without responding. He was astute and correctly guessed that the king had become enamoured of Satyavati, and they had been alone together before his return. Poor though he was, he was at an advantageous position. He bowed low to the king and said, 'Mighty King! I am honoured by your proposal. There can be no worthier groom than you for her in this entire world. However, I am bound to tell you the truth. Satyavati is not born of me. She has come from the sea. I found her when I cut open the belly of a huge fish that we had caught. I took her for a gift from the gods. Because she came from the stomach of a fish, an odour of fish surrounded her and I named her Matsyagandhi. Luckily for her, she obtained the blessings of a sage and this odour changed into a pleasing fragrance with his boon. After this change, I consulted astrologers to get her married. It has been prophesied that she will become queen and her children will rule a kingdom. Sire, I know that your son, Devavrata will be the next ruler of Hastinapur. How can I give my daughter to you? According to the prophecy I must wait for a king who will make her his queen and let her children ascend the throne. Sire, this is not possible with you. I humbly request you to take back your proposal because I want to secure the future of my grandchildren that the prophecy has guaranteed.'

King Shantanu was crestfallen and returned to his palace.

Shantanu lost his usual cheerful self. He became depressed and disinterested in life. Devavrata noticed the drastic change and tried to find out the cause. When he couldn't, he asked his father what was weighing on his mind but King Shantanu evaded his questions. Devavrata told his father, 'I am worried about you. If you do not share your problems with me, I will investigate myself and solve the problem that has taken over your peace of mind. Bless me father so that I succeed.'

King Shantanu seemed not to hear and Devavrata left the palace more concerned. In no time Devavrata found out that King Shantanu had been in this state since his return from a meeting with the chief of the fishermen. Devavrata immediately approached the chieftain, and telling him about his father's despondency, asked him to relate all that happened between them. The chieftain revealed the king's proposal of marriage, the prophecy, and the reason for his rejection of the proposal. Devavrata realized his father could not marry Satyavati because Devavrata would be the next king by the law of primogeniture. And the fisherman would not consent to the marriage till he made sure that his future grandchild would inherit the throne. There was only one way out—if prince Devavrata himself renounced the throne for some reason.

Devavrata loved his father and wanted Shantanu to be happy. He therefore solemnly declared to the chieftain, 'I renounce my claim to the throne. Satyavati's children will inherit the kingdom. I give you my word. Now accept my father's proposal.'

On hearing this, the fisherman was mighty pleased but crafty as he was, he wanted to get the most out of the situation. He replied with apparent worry, 'Sir! I know you will live up to your promise. But what of your children, and their progeny? How can we know that they will accept your vow and carry it out in future?'

In response to this Devavrata had to take another vow. In a firm voice he said, 'Holding the Panchabhuuta or five elements—*prithvi* 'earth', *ap* 'water', *tejas* 'fire', *vaayu* 'wind', *aakaasha* 'space'—as witnesses to my vow, I declare that I shall never marry. I assure you and your daughter that I shall remain a *brahmachari* (bachelor) all my life and serve the kingdom of Hastinapur.'

Hearing these tremendously self-sacrificial vows, the gods themselves appeared in the sky and showered flowers on Devavrata. They gave him the name 'Bhisma'—the one of terrible vow. The chieftain agreed now to the marriage and Devavrata went to King Shantanu with the good news. Shantanu was overwhelmed by the sacrifice made by his son. Though he was very happy that Satyavati would be his and once again he would have a queen by his side, his joy was overcast with remorse that his son's life had been ruined for his bliss. He embraced his son and with great emotion, said, 'My dear Devavrata! You have made a great sacrifice for my sake. This onerous self-sacrifice will forever be known and revered as *Bhisma-pratijnna*. I bless that your fame will remain undiminished till the end of time. I am proud of you and give you the boon that you shall have the power to choose the time of your death. You cannot be killed unless you yourself wish for it. It is the boon of *icchaamarana*.'

And so it was that the eighth Vasu was born to lead a mortal life as Gaangeya, the son of Gangaa, who grew up as Prince Devavrata, the eighth son of King Shantanu, and later came to be known far and wide as Bhisma.

chapter 4

Satyavati's Progeny—Chitrangada and Vichitraveerya

Devavrata, now called Bhisma, was not happy with his father's boons for he knew that his life would be a long one with much suffering. He also realized that there was no escape, as he had to live through the results of his actions in his previous life. Bhisma had been told about his birth, his earlier life as one of the AshtaVasus and of Vasistha's curse when he had visited Gangaa after taking his great vows.

The marriage of King Shantanu and Satyavati was celebrated with regal pomp and splendour. However, the people of the kingdom of Hastinapur were not happy with this turn of events. They felt that Bhisma's right had been unjustly snatched from him and did not have any faith that Satyavati's progeny would be able rulers in comparison to Bhisma. People were also upset that King Shantanu had chosen a commoner—a mere fisherwoman, and of unknown lineage at that—as his queen, whereas their erstwhile queen had been the divine and beauteous Gangaa. But as time passed people realized that though Bhisma would not sit on the throne, he would be the all-powerful influence on the king of Hastinapur; he would take all decisions and rule, if only by proxy.

After a few years, Satyavati bore Shantanu two sons; the elder one was named Chitrangada and the younger one, Vichitraveerya. Shantanu was quite old by then, hence Bhisma was the father figure to Chitrangada and Vichitraveerya. He brought them up with love and care and taught them all the skills they needed as princes. When the children were still young, Shantanu passed away. Satyavati began ruling the kingdom as regent while Bhisma administered the day to day affairs. Since Bhisma was at the helm, the kingdom prospered and there was peace and amity. The neighbouring kingdoms did not attack though there was no king on the throne, for fear of Bhisma.

When Chitrangada came of age, he was duly installed on the throne of Hastinapur. However, he did not rule for long. In the short span of time, being a brilliant warrior, he expanded his kingdom battling many of the neighbouring kings. After this expansion, Bhisma decided to travel to the newly acquired areas to address the concerns of the people there. So he set out after advising Chitrangada on how to manage the kingdom in his absence.

Unfortunately for Chitrangada, no sooner had Bhisma left, than a Gandharva came to his court and challenged him to a fight. The Gandharva stood shouting outside the palace,

'Who is it who has dared to name himself with my name? I will not tolerate this. Only one person can exist in this world with one name and that will be me. I will destroy anyone who has used my name. Come out O King! And fight with me.'

Hearing him, Chitrangada came out with his courtiers. He saw a huge giant of a man, fuming with anger but regal and good-looking. He asked the stranger, 'Who are you and why are you here? I am Chitrangada, the ruler of Hastinapur'.

The Gandharva screamed, 'I am Chitrangada, the king of the Gandharvas. How dare you use my name! I have come to kill you! You cannot have the same name and yet be alive. Come and fight me'.

The king's courtiers advised him to play for time and await Bhisma's return. They apprised him of the folly of accepting a challenge from a stranger, especially as Gandharvas were known for their magical powers. The Gandharva had chosen to come when Bhisma was absent—this could be a clever strategy. However, Chitrangada, concerned with his honour and pride, did not pay heed to their words. He accepted the challenge and there was a long drawn duel between the two Chitrangadas—one a human, physically strong and well versed in warfare, the other a Gandharva, ferocious and possessing magical powers in addition to strength and valour. The king of Hastinapur could not withstand the two pronged attack of the Gandharva—physical and the use of magic—and died. Strangely, the Gandharva did not attack the people and laughing, simply left the place.

Hearing this news, Bhisma rushed back to Hastinapur.

He was broken hearted when he heard the details from the inconsolable Satyavati. Bhisma cursed himself for having left the capital but now there was no way he could undo what had happened. Since the throne could not remain without a king, Satyavati counselled Bhisma to crown her second son Vichitraveerya immediately. As Chitrangada had no heirs, Vichitraveerya became the king of Hastinapur and Bhisma began training him on the ways of good governance.

Thus the promise made by Bhisma to the fisherman chief that his grandchildren would be rulers, was fulfilled and both sons of Satyavati sat on the throne of Hastinapur.

chapter 5

A Clash of Vows

After Chitrangada's death, Satyavati remained depressed and spent a long time in solitude. Bhisma not only took care of the kingdom but also gave parental support to Vichitraveerya. Soon Vichitraveerya came of age. One day, while watching Vichitraveerya practice fencing, Satyavati called Bhisma and said, 'O Prince, you have transformed Vichitraveerya into a strong and capable person fit to rule the kingdom, and I cannot thank you enough for this. You have not only kept your vow but have also taken up responsibilities that are not truly yours. Without you, Devavrata, I do not know what would have happened. Now I think it is time for Vichitraveerya to marry. I believe that one should rule with his consort beside him. The king of Kasi is going to perform a *swayamvara* (an event wherein a girl chooses a groom from among assembled suitors, sometimes based on a test of valour) for his daughters. Vichitraveerya, though valorous, cannot yet handle the numerous suitors and may not be able to win the contest to get a bride. Could you not go to the swayamvara and win a bride for him? I know I have no right to ask this of you, but it would please me very much. Since you have done so much for him, would you not wish to see him married as well?'

Bhisma replied, 'Mother, I am only fulfilling my vow. I have not done anything for which you need to express gratitude or be indebted. My vow was for my father's happiness and even after he is gone, I will work towards what would have pleased him. Yes, it is time for Vichitraveerya to marry. The princesses of Kasi are acclaimed for their beauty and virtue, and will make suitable brides for my brother. I will go to Kasi as you wish and bring back daughters-in-law for you.'

Satyavati was very happy with his decision but reminded him thus: 'Devavrata, I need to mention this. The king of Kasi has not invited the prince of Hastinapur for the swayamvara. Thus you will be going there uninvited. I wonder if this is appropriate.'

Bhisma roared, 'Mother, the king of Kasi has insulted us by deliberately ignoring Hastinapur and I am eager to avenge it. The best way to teach him a lesson would be to abduct the three princesses and perform a Gandharva wedding (a wedding wherein only the consent of the bride and the groom is required, and the five elements of nature, the *panchabhuutas*, are its witnesses) with the crown prince. That would be a suitable reply to the Kasi king's insult. I will go there and return victorious.'

The kings assembled in the court of the ruler of Kasi were

surprised when Bhisma strode into the palace. They began murmuring among themselves, 'Why is Bhisma here? He has taken a vow of lifelong celibacy. Has the beauty of the Kasi princesses made him give up his promise to his father?'

Bhisma ignored the speculations and strode up to the king. 'O King, I do not come here seeking a bride for myself,' he said. 'I have come here on behalf of my brother Vichitraveerya. The princesses will become the queens of Hastinapur.' Then he turned to the assembled royalty. 'But if any of you wishes to stop this marriage, he will have to fight me.' Having said this, he approached the three princesses Amba, Ambika, and Ambalika, and forced them to follow him into his chariot which was waiting just outside the palace. The shocked princesses cried out to their father who had slumped in his throne, tears rolling down his face, knowing that he could not fight Bhisma to protect his daughters. Bhisma carried away the princesses and the swayamvara sabha broke up in chaos.

The kings who had come for the swayamvara were furious. Though they knew Bhisma was a great warrior they felt that their insult had to be avenged and that their collective strength would enable them to overcome Bhisma. Immediately they set off in pursuit of Bhisma and the three princesses. They called out to Bhisma, 'Stop this injustice. Fight us and if you win, you may take the princesses. We will not accept this quietly.'

Bhisma turned his chariot to face them, his face creased with a triumphant smile. A brief war of sorts ensued. The kings were no match for Bhisma's prowess though they were many in number. One by one they fell to the ground. One king however gave stiff resistance. He was King Salva. The fight between Salva and Bhisma was fierce. After a long drawn fight Bhisma destroyed the chariot and horses of Salva and took aim to end his life. At that moment, the eldest princess of Kasi, Amba, fell at Bhisma's feet and begged him to spare the life of the valiant warrior. Bhisma acceded to her request. Seeing the valiant King Salva's fall, the remaining kings conceded defeat and returned to their kingdoms.

In Hastinapur, Bhisma presented the three Kasi princesses to his mother Satyavati and asked her to make preparations for a grand wedding. Seeing one of them weeping, Satyavati approached her and asked, 'My dear, what is your name? Why are you crying? Did my son Bhisma do something wrong to you? Have no fear and tell me, and I will do whatever it takes to wipe your tears.'

The princess sobbed, 'O Queen Mother! I am Amba, the eldest daughter of the king of Kasi. I have been carried away by your son by force and against my will. I am not desirous of marrying anyone other than King Salva. We, King Salva and I, have been in love for a long time. I had promised to garland him in the swayamvara. Since I have already accepted him as my husband in my heart, I cannot think of marrying anyone else. I could not tell Bhisma all this in my father's court. Please help me.'

Hearing this, Bhisma replied, 'I was unaware of this, Princess Amba. If only you had told me this before,

I would have acted differently. But do not worry, I will make arrangements for you to be escorted with due respect to King Salva so that you can marry him. I will not force you to marry Vichitraveerya.'

Princess Amba was duly sent to the court of King Salva. However, Salva refused to accept her, saying that he had been defeated in battle by Bhisma who had abducted the princesses, and after being thus shamed, he could not accept Amba as his wife. Salva asked Amba to return to Hastinapur. Brokenhearted, princess Amba returned to Hastinapur and asked Vichitraveerya to marry her. But Vichtiraveerya refused, saying he would not marry a woman who had declared having already accepted another as her husband. Amba was now in a pitiable state, having been spurned by the one she loved and the man who had been ready to marry her. There seemed to be only one way out—Bhisma.

In this pitiful state Amba beseeched Bhisma to save her honour by marrying her since now no one else would, and returning to her father was out of the question after what had happened. But Bhisma, bound as he was by his vow, would not even think of violating it by agreeing to the marriage, though he sympathized with her plight.

All doors were shut for Amba and her grief turned into fury. Bhisma was the root cause of her devastation. A distraught Amba could hold herself no longer and shouted at him, 'When you had taken the vow of never being with a woman, what gave you the right to abduct me? How could you come in place of your brother to the swayamvara? Was that honourable? Your brother would never have won us and we would have had a chance to choose our husbands. It is *you* who has ruined my life, Bhisma. It is because of *your* actions that I have nowhere to go. Kill me now or fight me.'

Bhisma refused gently. 'I am helpless because of my vow of celibacy, *devi*. And being a warrior, I will never fight a woman'.

Nothing could prevail over his decision. After all, he was Bhisma—the one of onerous vows.

And so it was that princess Amba, who solely blamed Bhisma for ruining her life, left the palace with a vow on her lips: 'I will avenge this someday.'

chapter 6

A Vow of Vengeance and a Boon

Princess Amba left Hastinapur seething with fury at Bhisma. It never occurred to Amba that Salva was equally to blame for her situation as he had failed to defend her against Bhisma at the swayamvar sabha and had rejected her when she had come to him later.

Amba travelled through dense forests and finally reached the hermitage of Sage Parashurama. He listened to her tale of woe and agreed to help her. Now Sage Parashurama was no ordinary sage; we need to go into his past to know who he really was.

Parashurama's father, Jamadagni, had been cruelly killed by King Kartaviryarjuna when Parashurama was away. On returning, he found his mother Renuka Devi wailing over the dead body of his father. Incensed, Parashurama made a terrible vow—to wipe out all the Kshatriyas from the face of the earth! This was at a time when the Kshatriyas as a race had descended to the depths of decadence and degradation.

King Kartaviryarjuna was an epitome of such rulers and his was the first head to be cut off by Parashurama's battle-axe. Parashurama travelled around the world twenty-one times, to carry out his vow of killing every single Kshatriya. Blood flowed in rivers and at last the vow was fulfilled. That is when he had retired from the world, immersing himself in intense penance, pursuing austerities in a secluded hermitage. The vengeful Parashurama eventually turned into a venerable sage.

Sage Parashurama was Bhisma's guru and felt that he could convince his pupil to do justice to Princess Amba. He approached Bhisma and talked to him at length trying to convince Bhisma that what he had done was wrong and that Princess Amba's life would be ruined. Bhisma, however, was bound by the vow of celibacy he had made to ensure the happiness of his father, and stood firm on it. It is said that the brave do not leave the righteous path ever (*nyaayaad pathah pravicalanti padam na dhiiraah*) and it was true in the case of Bhisma. But Sage Parashurama, unable to persuade Bhisma to marry Princess Amba, became furious and challenged Bhisma to a duel. The fight raged for several days with no clear winner as both teacher and pupil were equal combatants. Moreover, Bhisma had the boon of his father by which nobody could kill him. In the end, Sage Parashurama called truce and advised Amba thus: 'My child, I am unable to get you justice. I cannot win over Bhisma nor kill him as he is protected by his father's boon. Forget all this and return home.'

But this was not acceptable to Amba as she had nowhere to go.

Princess Amba decided to pray to the gods, asking for help. She went into the forest and began severe austerities for Siva's boon. For twelve long years Amba focused only on this. Such was her intensity, that Siva appeared before her and asked her what she wanted. This was exactly what Amba had waited for, for twelve years. Amba fell at his feet and said, 'O Lord! You know all that has befallen me in my life. I seek revenge against Bhisma. I am so consumed by my desire for revenge that I am unable to reconcile myself to an ordinary life. There is only one thing I desire—to kill Bhisma. Grant me the ability to do that.'

Siva said, 'I am pleased with your penance, but what you ask for is not possible. In this life and in this form, you will not be able to kill Bhisma since women are not allowed to participate in war. And without fighting Bhisma, you cannot kill him in a fair manner. So my boon to you will be for your next life. I bless that you will be responsible for Bhisma's death. You will be born to King Drupada of Panchala and by my boon, you shall remember this life of yours. Because of this memory, you will be able to avenge yourself when the opportunity presents itself.'

Having given his boons, Siva disappeared. Amba was overjoyed that she had achieved her purpose. But she did not want to live a life that had lost all meaning. So, instead of waiting for death, she created a funeral pyre and immolated herself to be released from her present body and be ready to be born again to avenge herself.

However, since she had ended her life unnaturally, before her lifecycle was completed, Amba was born again as a woman to complete the period she had sought to cut short. According to Siva's boon, she later transformed herself into a man to fight Bhisma, and was finally able to quench her thirst for vengeance.

But that is another story.

chapter 7

Sage Vedavyasa Sires the Bharata Clan

Unlike Amba, her sisters Ambika and Ambalika were happy at being chosen to be the brides of Vichitraveerya, king of Hastinapur. The whole kingdom witnessed festivities for more than a week. Ambika and Ambalika spent about seven years with Vichitraveerya but neither of them could beget an heir. They spent their time in prayer and performed various rituals and austerities to beget children but to no avail. Then Vichitraveerya was struck by tuberculosis and died shortly thereafter.

With no heir to the Hastinapur throne, Satyavati began spending sleepless nights. She did not know what to do. King Shantanu was dead and so were both her sons. One day she approached Bhisma thus: 'My son, I have been the cause of your sorrow right from the beginning. I wed your father only after you gave up your right to the throne and took the vow of celibacy to ensure that my sons ascend the Hastinapur throne. Now I realize that I am paying for those sins. Both my sons are dead and the kingdom is heirless. Who will now rule Hastinapur? I beseech you, Bhisma, to provide a solution. Please marry Ambika and Ambalika and sire children. You have always said that the throne of Hastinapur takes precedence over your personal life. Now is the time for you to save the kingdom of Hastinapur from sure ruin.'

Bhisma's face registered shock and disgust when he heard Satyavati suggesting he marry his brother's wives to beget heirs to the throne. But he remained firm in his refusal. Satyavati argued with him, begged him, and finally ordered him as the regent of Hastinapur, but Bhisma refused to budge from his vow of celibacy. Seeing his mother's helplessness, Bhisma sought the answer in tomes of *raja dharma* and suggested that the *niyoga* method be used to further the lineage. In ancient times, a woman could seek the help of any suitable person to bear a child if she was widowed childless or her husband was incapable of fatherhood. Usually a revered person or learned scholar would do this for the sake of Dharma, considering it a duty and not for pleasure. Niyoga was primarily used to continue a lineage.

Faced with an heirless kingdom, Satyavati remembered the son she had got as a boon from Sage Parashara. She confided in Bhisma about the birth of Vedavyasa before her marriage to King Shantanu, and his promise that he would come in her time of need. Bhisma agreed that Vyasa was the most suitable person for siring the future heir of Hastinapur. Satyavati called out to Vyasa, and lo and behold,

Sage Vyasa appeared before her as he had promised. It took all of Satyavati's powers of persuasion to coax Sage Vyasa and her daughters-in-law to agree to niyoga. Sage Vyasa contended that it was not a good time to bear children as the stars were not favourable and he was in the middle of austerities, but Satyavati was in no mood to listen. Finally, she commanded her son to obey her as his mother, and Vyasa had to acquiesce.

On the first night, Satyavati sent Ambika to Vedavyasa's chamber. Vedavyasa had been in the forest for several years performing intense meditation and austerities. To a princess, he looked unkempt and fierce. Ambika was so frightened to be with him that she closed her eyes and kept them shut throughout the night. The next night Satyavati sent Ambalika to Vedavyasa so that she too would beget a child. Ambalika, nervous as she was, paled on seeing Vedavyasa's frightening visage. All blood left her face and she remained thus throughout the night.

Vedavyasa told Satyavati how her daughters-in-law had behaved and the consequences that would inevitably follow. He told his mother that Ambika's son would be born blind while Ambalika's son would be bloodless and pale in appearance. When Satyavati learnt of all this she begged Vedavyasa to help beget another son. Satyavati asked Ambika to go to Vedavyasa's chamber again but Ambika feared Vedavyasa so much that she sent her maid instead. The maid thought it was her great fortune to bear the child of such a venerable sage. She did not fear Vedavyasa but felt grateful and honoured to be with him. Vedavyasa blessed her with a winsome child, intelligent and wise. He grew up to be called Vidura.

Whan Vedavyasa told Satyavati everything, Satyavati was enraged. She wanted to send for Ambika and chastise her for having not only failed in her duties, but also for deceiving a sage. 'How dare she disobey me', she raged. 'I will also banish the maid for having betrayed me. I cannot have a maid bring up a royal offspring in this palace, knowing that it is your child', she fumed.

Seeing his mother so distraught, Vedavyasa opened up. 'There is a reason for all this', he said. 'First listen to the story of this third son of mine—who he is, why he is going to be born here and what he is destined to do.'

And so begins another story of another lifetime...

Once upon a time there lived a sage called Mandavya. He had studied long and hard and attained great knowledge. He spent his days in penance and austerities in a forest on the outskirts of a kingdom.

One night, a group of thieves entered the king's palace and grabbed whatever they could lay their hands on. On their way out they tripped over a soldier, and the noise woke up the others, who gave chase. The thieves ran into the forest where Sage Mandavya sat meditating under a tree for three days, having entered the state of *samadhi*. He saw the robbers enter his hermitage but remained aloof, absorbed in meditation. The thieves hid their loot in the hermitage and made themselves scarce, deciding to come back for the booty once the soldiers chasing them had left the forest. Soon the soldiers neared the hermitage and seeing the sage, the commander asked him if he had seen the thieves. But before the sage could emerge out of *samadhi* and reply, some of the men espied the booty inside the hermitage, and rushing to the commander said 'Sir! He is a rogue and hence is silent. He must be hand in glove with the thieves. We have found the stolen goods in his hermitage!'

The commander reported to the king what had taken place, giving the impression that Sage Mandavya was the chief of the robbers and the others had escaped while the leader had been caught. The enraged king ordered that the sage be impaled for his guilt and the order was speedily carried out. Sage Mandavya however had not reached the end of his life since he was still in the meditative trance when impaled on a spear. He remained alive by the power of yoga.

The next day the news of the king's order spread far and wide. All those who lived in the vicinity came to Sage Mandavya's hermitage and were shocked to see him impaled on a spear. They hastened to the palace and urged the king to withdraw his order since the victim was not a robber but a sage. The king was surprised and hurried to the forest. Seeing Sage Mandavya impaled, he panicked. He ordered the sage to be taken down from the spear but while doing so, the spear broke and the head of the spear remained embedded in the sage's body. The king fell at the sage's feet and begged for forgiveness. Sage Mandavya forgave him because he knew that the king had unwittingly committed a mistake, and he had only done what had been ordained by Yamadharmaraya.

So Sage Mandavya approached Yamadharmaraya, who was seated on his throne, dispensing justice, and asked 'Why was I subject to such horrendous torture? I am a jnaani and understand that every person has to reap what he has sown in his previous lives. I know of no sins that I have committed in this life or my previous lives that would invite such a punishment. Tell me, what action of mine from my previous births has led you to mete out this unjust punishment to me?'

On seeing the furious sage, Yamadharmaraya, rose from his throne and with folded hands said, 'I have not meted out injustice. You have indeed sinned in your last birth. You have killed flies by swatting them and piercing them with sharp twigs. As a result you had to undergo the pain of impalement. As you are aware, all deeds, small and large, good and bad, do set in motion a resultant chain of events that one has to endure.'

The sage requested for the ability to watch those actions of his previous birth and Mandavya saw himself swatting flies as a child. This made him boil with rage and he thundered, 'You are aware that a child has no knowledge of good and evil. Sins committed by children below the age of fourteen belong to their parents. Moreover, how can you assign a punishment far disproportionate to the so-called crime?'

And in his fury, Sage Mandavya pronounced a curse on Yamadharmaraya: 'May you be born on the earth as a mortal and suffer the consequences of every action of yours, small or big, good or bad. Only then will you understand and attain the sense of justice and proportion which you lack now.'

As a result of the sage's curse, Yamadharmaraya had to be born as Vidura, son of the maidservant whom Ambika had sent to Vedavyasa for niyoga. The third child of Vedavyasa was, therefore, no ordinary mortal! Vidura was a great soul, wise and just. He was also spiritually enlightened but being born as a maid's offspring, he was never given the respect he deserved.

And as a consequence of Satyavati's undue haste to get heirs for the throne of Hastinapur, and her refusal to follow Vedavyasa's advice to await an auspicious time, both the princes born were flawed—Dhritarashtra born blind, and the other, Pandu, born strangely pale.

chapter 8

Sahasrakavaci, the Mighty Demon King

Dambhodbhava was a mighty demon of the Treta Yuga. Like all asuras, he wanted to become immortal. When Vishnu had assumed the avatar of a '*Kurma*' (tortoise) and the oceans had been churned, the nectar of immortality that came forth was consumed by the gods, or devas, to become immortal. Most of the demons who were bereft of the nectar made efforts to achieve immortality through penance and prayers. But since they wanted to achieve this goal of theirs only to harass humans and gods, they never fully succeeded. Dambhodbhava performed severe austerities right from his childhood. He prayed to Surya, the Sun god, for several years. Pleased with his devotion, Surya appeared before him one day, 'My child Dambhodbhava, I am touched by your devotion and penance. Ask me for a boon and it shall be granted'.

Without hesitation Dambhodbhava said, 'O Lord! I want to become all-powerful! I want to be invincible. I want to live forever and never die. Grant me such a boon.'

Surya smiled and said, 'You ask for what cannot be given. Everyone who is born has to die (*jaatasya maranam dhruvam*). Immortality is out of question. It cannot be granted to anyone. Ask me for something else.'

Dambhodbhava thought for some time. He decided that if he asked for protection against Indra and the gods, he would automatically become invincible. 'O Lord, grant that I become invincible and give me a long life. Let me not die at the hands of Indra and the gods. Give me a thousand-layered armour, each layer of which should be equal to one life. That means, I want a thousand lives before I die. Grant me the boon that only those who have performed penance for a thousand years will be able to break an armour. And whoever breaks my armour should also die. Lastly, grant the boon that if ever I am in dire need, you will come for my protection and do your best to save me.' With this long winded request Dambhodbhava thought he would become immortal.

Surya did not like what he heard. He felt it was equivalent to granting immortality. A thousand lives would have to be sacrificed to break through the thousand armours. However, he was bound by honour to give the boon. 'Granted!' said Surya and disappeared as quickly as he had appeared, before Dambhodbhava could ask for anything more.

Dambhodbhava was overjoyed. He felt he had duped the god into granting him immortality by way of asking for a thousand lives. He believed that none could fight through so many armours and kill him. He went to Patala—the Underworld—and began his rule of the Asuras. Like many before him and many more after him, he became arrogant with power and cruel, attacking kingdoms and killing people mercilessly. He even attacked Swargaloka—Heaven—and dethroned Indra and the gods. He crowned himself the King of Heavens. People addressed him as Sahasrakavaci or one with a thousand armours.

Sahasrakavaci's atrocities continued for several years and people began praying to Vishnu, the Protector, to save them from Sahasrakavaci. The gods, led by Indra, approached Brahma for help. Brahma said, 'Only Vishnu can help you in this. Surya cannot kill his own devotee. Also the boons given by him have made Sahasrakavaci almost invincible. Ask Vishnu to take two forms as he needs to perform austerities and fight the demon simultaneously. Otherwise, it is impossible to overcome Sahasrakavaci.'

Thus advised by Brahma, Indra led the Devas to Vaikuntha—the heavenly abode of Lord Vishnu and his consort Goddess Lakshmi. Indra said, 'O Lord! Have mercy on your children. Surya has armed the demon Sahasrakavaci with his blessings and boons. Only you can protect us from his cruelty. Please come to our rescue.'

Vishnu replied, 'This is no easy task and will take a lot of time. It will take years to penetrate through each armour of Sahasrakavaci. I must take two forms—one to perform penance to Shankara for strength, and the other to fight the demon. The two forms will take turns to fight and do penance. Once the battle begins, all of you will be free from Sahasrakavaci's reign as he will be engaged with me and in his absence you, Indra, can get back your kingdom.'

Accordingly, Vishnu was born to Dharma, a *manasaputra* of Brahma, and his wife Muurti, both of whom were his devotees. He took the form of twins named Nara and Narayana who grew up in the ashrama learning various skills including warcraft. Nara and Narayana were staying in the forests of Badrinath when Sahasrakavaci attacked that area. The other sages in the ashrama requested Nara and Narayana to save them. Together the duo challenged Sahasrakavaci to a duel. 'O King of the three realms, we wish to test your strength and courage. We do not want to spill the blood of your soldiers. We challenge you to a one-to-one combat.'

Sahasrakavaci laughed and said, 'You are two persons wanting to fight with a single person, how is that a one-to one? That is against the rules of war. Who are you and why have you come here to fight me?'

Nara said, 'You are a mighty king! I am Vishnu, the sustainer of the universe. I have taken two forms because I cannot win against you easily since you are favoured by Surya. But we shall follow the rules of war. Only one of us will fight you at any point in time. In the meantime, the other will do penance. When the person fighting you gets tired he will take rest and the other will fight you. You are endowed with a thousand armours! You are a great warrior! Give us an opportunity to test your valour.'

Sahasrakavaci was taken in by Nara's words. He felt

immensely proud that even Vishnu had to take two forms in order to fight him. Dambhodbava felt that Vishnu was not aware that the person who broke his armour would die immediately. Therefore, at the most Nara and Narayana would break two of his armours. He would still possess 998 armours. He felt safe in agreeing to Vishnu's request and the battle began. First Nara engaged Sahasrakavaci in combat—sometimes wrestling, sometimes with a weapon. Narayana sat down for penance. At the end of a thousand years, Nara was able to cut out one layer of armour and fell dead, while Sahasrakavaci remained as energetic as ever. Narayana came out of his austerities and chanted the Sanjeevini *mantra* which revived Nara, who then sat down to perform penance. The Sanjeevini mantra had been taught to Vishnu by Shankara and it could revive a dead person. Narayana then started fighting Dambhodbhava. Though Dambhodbhava realized that he had been tricked into combat by Vishnu, he could not back off. In this manner Nara and Narayana fought for thousands and thousands of years cutting out one layer of protective cover after another every thousand years.

Aeons rolled by. Nara would fight for a thousand years while Narayana performed austerities and then Nara would perform austerities for a thousand years while Narayana would fight in his place. This continued relentlessly and finally Sahasrakavaci was down to the last armour. It was time to begin the last round and Nara got up from his austerities to relieve Narayana. But it was not yet over for Sahasrakavaci. He now knew that death was not far away and he was no longer immortal. He decided to change tactics. He remembered that he could ask for Surya's help and save himself. He left the battlefield and rushed to Surya, pleading for protection. Nara came chasing Sahasrakavaci and was confronted by Surya who begged him not to kill Sahasrakavaci as the demon was his devotee and had sought his refuge.

In the meantime, it was time for *pralaya*—the conclusion of the Treta Yuga. Vishnu had to enter cosmic slumber. Brahma appeared and addressed all of them. 'This is the end of this yuga and all must return unto *Brahman*. However Sahasrakavaci, you still have one life and one set of armour left. Hence I ordain you to be born again in the next yuga—the Dwapara Yuga. Nara and Narayana shall also incarnate themselves and fight you in the new yuga with different methods and a different measure of time. For all the sins you have committed in this life, you will suffer hardships throughout your next life'.

And in that moment Sahasrakavaci's rebirth and the course of his next life was sealed.

Then Brahma turned to Surya. 'Since you have given boons to a wicked person and despite his actions you have protected him so long, you, Surya, will not be able to protect your protégé in his next life. He shall be born of you but will act of his own will and reap what he has sown'.

And in a twinkling everything vanished, swallowed by the waters of Pralaya as the yuga came to an end.

chapter 9

Durvasa's Boon: The Story of Kunti

Shurasena was a Yadava clan leader and the father of Prithaa and Vasudeva. Vasudeva married Devaki, the daughter of King Ugrasena and the sister of Kamsa. Vasudeva and Devaki became parents of Krishna, the divine incarnation of Vishnu. Prithaa, therefore, became the paternal aunt of Krishna. Shurasena had a cousin called Kuntibhoja, and the two were very close to each other. Kuntibhoja had been childless for long and often expressed his sadness to Shurasena. Shurasena was so moved by his cousin's misery that even before the birth of his daughter, he had promised Kuntibhoja his firstborn. So a few years after Prithaa's birth, Shurasena gave her away to Kuntibhoja. And thus Prithaa became Kunti.

Under Kuntibhoja's loving care, Kunti grew up into a comely girl, not a beauty as most princesses are often believed to be, but a paragon of fortitude and virtue. Kuntibhoja showered her with much love and Kunti loved her foster father as she would have loved the real one.

When Kunti was sixteen years old, the irascible but powerful sage Durvasa visited Kuntibhoja. Durvasa was universally feared for his temper and his proclivity to curse. Kuntibhoja welcomed him with much trepidation saying, 'I am honoured to have this opportunity to serve you, Sire. Tell me how may I please you.' Sage Durvasa, pleased with the humility of the king, said, 'I would like to spend some days in prayer in your kingdom. You may make arrangements for it. I also need someone to assist me.' Kuntibhoja thought it would be best for Kunti to take care of the sage. 'My daughter will be honoured to be of service to you,' he said. 'I am confident that she will serve you well during your stay with us.'

Kuntibhoja's faith in his daughter was vindicated; the sage was extremely pleased with the fervour and devotion with which Kunti attended to his every need. Despite the sage's often unreasonable requests at odd hours, Kunti served him with dedication and patience. Eventually after a few months, he called Kunti. 'I will be leaving shortly', he said. 'I am pleased with you and would like to bless you with a boon for good progeny.' So saying, Sage Durvasa gave to her a special mantra. 'This mantra has great power. When you recite it, any god you desire will be bound by this mantra to appear before you and grant you progeny. So use the mantra wisely and with caution. I repeat, it will bring any god you wish to your presence.'

It is probable that with his yogic knowledge he knew that Kunti would not be able to conceive children with her husband, and thus had given her the boon for offsprings before he left.

One fine morning young Kunti was standing at a window when she chanced to look towards the sun. She was filled with fascination at his all-pervading radiance and without thought, she uttered the mantra. The next instant Surya stood before her in her chamber, in all his regal splendour. Kunti was struck with awe at the sight but quickly regained her composure. She bowed to Surya with folded hands, her voice a slight quiver, 'Please return to your abode in the heavens, Dev, and forgive me, for I spoke the words without thinking. I apologize for my errant behaviour.' And then the full import of the boon struck her and she cried out, 'I am yet unmarried, O Lord; I cannot bear your child! I have been foolish and careless—please have pity on me and return.'

But Surya was bound by the power of the mantra. 'Fair maiden, I understand your predicament but I am helpless, bound as I am by Sage Durvasa's mantra. You may however, rest assured that you will remain a virgin despite the fact that a son will be born to you.' And thus was Karna born of Surya, divinely handsome and resplendent like his father. From birth his chest was covered with a golden *kavaca*—magical armour, and his ears bore a pair of golden *kundalas*, or earrings, as brilliant as his father's radiance. These of course were the vestiges of the armour of his previous birth as Sahasrakacavi, that nobody in Dwapara Yuga knew of.

Kunti wept as she held the baby in her arms, tears of

motherly love mixed with tears of shame and misgivings. 'What will happen now?' the miserable girl thought. 'How shall I face my father? I have failed him, my God, what did I do! He will not be able to face the world because of me. How will I explain all this to him? How can I bring infamy to the royal household?' she fretted. 'The only solution possible is to get rid of the baby!'

And thus Kunti compounded one misdeed with a greater one. In the darkness of the night she placed the baby in a basket and set it afloat in the Ganga, setting off a chain of events she could never have imagined.

As Kunti let go of her bundle of joy, she unknowingly embraced a lifetime of regret and sorrow, which only grew with time as the future unfolded. Unlike Satyavati, Kunti never accepted Karna as her firstborn until the great war had ended. Satyavati had not only proclaimed to all the boon she had received from Sage Parashara, she accepted Vyasa as her son and took his help whenever needed. Kunti, despite the example of Satyavati before her, behaved in a totally different manner. First, she did not use the boon as she should have, and having used it, was ashamed of it, lacking the courage to accept Karna as her son either at his birth or later when the opportunity arose. Despite the boon being the same, the trajectories of their lives were totally different, reaping completely different harvests.

When Kunti came of age, her father arranged a swayamvara for her, inviting suitors from far and near. Her qualities and character had brought her fame and many arrived at the swayamvara, desirous of being the chosen one. Pandu, prince of Hastinapur, representing the Kura lineage was chosen by Kunti. The wedding was solemnized and she accompanied her husband to Hastinapur.

chapter 10

Karna—A Boon-child Is Cursed

Surya's boon child, cast away by princess Kunti, was found by Adiratha—personal charioteer of Dhritarashtra, King of Hastinapur and the elder brother of Pandu. Adiratha and his wife Radha, being childless, were overcome with joy and raised the child as their own, never letting him know that he was a foundling. The child looked divine, with his golden kavacha and kundalas that were inseparable from his body. They christened him Vasusena. But he was more popular by his other names—Karna, Radheya (son of Radha), Aadhirathi (son of Adiratha) and Sutaputra (son of a charioteer). Sutaputra was used more as a taunt—and throughout his life Karna was shadowed by taunts.

Karna grew up into a strapping handsome youth with a strikingly noble appearance. He learnt the art of charioteering from Adiratha but he seemed to have a calling of his own. Karna wanted to reach out to the sun, he wanted to learn the art of battle and archery like a Kshatriya. He felt it in his genes, in his blood. He dreamt of being the greatest archer in the world but since he was a low caste charioteer's son, nobody would teach him the skills of a Kshatriya. He was taunted as Sutaputra and turned away by all teachers.

Karna approached Drona, who was the guru of the Kuru princes. Drona, who was suffering from his own complexities, refused to teach him saying that Karna was neither a prince nor a Kshatriya. Karna immediately responded 'Sir, I beg to differ. Aswathama is being taught by you and he is neither a prince nor a Kshatriya. A guru is revered as much for his impartiality and justice as for his knowledge. How then can you apply one rule for your son and another rule for me?' Drona became furious but remained silent even as Karna left the place.

Karna then approached the great Parashurama who had been the guru of Drona and even of Bhisma. (Bhisma, though a Kshatriya, had been accepted by Parashurama as a disciple on Gangaa's intervention.) Parashurama had traversed the earth twenty-one times to erase the very Kshatriya race, but later, overcome with disgust at the *syamantapancaka* or the five pools of blood that he himself had created, he had retired to the forests for penance.

Karna knew that this was his last chance to learn the art of warfare. When he bowed to Parashurama, the sage spoke thus: 'Your visage tells me that you belong to a noble lineage. I am sure you are aware that I do not teach Kshatriyas for the disaster that was wrought in my life. Are you a Kshatriya?' Karna immediately fell at his feet saying, 'O Great One! I am not a Kshatriya. Please accept me as your pupil.' Karna did not mention that he was a charioteer's son and strategically allowed Parashurama to mistake him for a Brahmin boy. Karna was thus accepted as a disciple by Parashurama. Karna spent several years under Parashurama's tutelage and learnt all the secrets of warfare with special focus on archery. He mastered the mantras and acquired divine powers and weapons whereby he could call upon the power of the gods while discharging weapons.

One day when Parashurama and Karna were returning to the hermitage after collecting firewood, Parashurama said, 'Karna, I am tired. I want to rest awhile.' Karna sat down in the shade of a large tree, and took his guru's head on his lap so that the sage could rest comfortably. After some time, an insect bit into Karna's thigh since he was immobile. The pain was unbearable but Karna did not utter a sound as he did not want to disturb his guru. He began bleeding and soon the warm blood reached Parashurama. This woke him up and he was horrified to see Karna bleeding. Karna said, 'Sire, please ignore this. I did not want to wake you up. I am sorry I failed.'

But Parashurama sat up with a start, saying, 'Your fortitude and tolerance makes me wonder. I cannot believe that a Brahmin boy can bear such pain without a word. You cannot belong to the Brahmin *varna*. You are a Kshatriya! Have you deceived me? Who are you? Tell me the truth before I curse you!' Karna was forced to tell him all about himself. Parashurama controlled his fury somewhat and said,

'I regret that society has been cruel to you. However, the fact that you have deceived your guru remains, and you will have to pay for it. By my curse, the very knowledge that you have gained from me by deceit will be forgotten at the time of your greatest need. Leave me now and return home.' A downcast Karna left his guru's ashrama and returned to Hastinapur.

On his way back, Karna was so immersed in his thoughts that he did not see a small girl walking with a pot of milk on her head. He dashed against her and her pot fell to the ground, spilling all the milk. The girl started weeping, afraid of the scolding she would receive because of the broken pot and spilt milk. Karna apologized and offered to get her a new pot of milk that she could take home. But the girl wailed saying, 'No, that will not do. My mother had asked me to get milk from the cow in that house. You have to retrieve the spilt milk from the ground.'

Karna tried his best to convince her of the unreasonableness of her request and when he could not do so, decided to demonstrate how it was impossible to do what she wanted. He took a fistful of earth where the milk had spilt and squeezed it. Not a drop of milk could he extract. Instead, a thunderous clap was followed by the appearance of a beautiful woman cringing with pain. As Karna's fingers loosened in astonishment and the fistful of earth fell off, the woman spoke: 'I am Bhoomi Devi, Mother to all beings on earth. You caused me great pain by your foolish action. What made you think that you can get milk by squeezing me? Such action is against the law of nature, and therefore, unpardonable. You have caused me grievous hurt and I will punish you by not helping you in your time of need. It will be an example for all who ravage me.'

Having earned two curses, a despondent Karna returned home.

In the final war, at the hour when Arjuna and Karna were engaged with each other, Krishna led their chariots into a slushy area on the battlefield and a wheel of Karna's chariot got critically stuck in the mud. Karna tried his best to get the wheel out so that he could move, and when his charioteer Shalya refused to help, Karna prayed to Bhoomidevi, asking for help. It was then that she reminded Karna of this incident and he realized the import of her curse.

Realizing that he would never be able to extricate the stuck wheel of his chariot, Karna raised his bow, ready to utter the mantra for a *divyastra*. In that critical moment, Parashurama's curse came true and Karna forgot all the divine mantras, rendering him helpless. And Surya, Karna's father, could not help him at his hour of greatest need because of Brahma's curse uttered in an earlier yuga.

Soon an arrow from Arjuna pierced him and Karna's life came to an end. Karna had lived through all his curses and was now free of them.

Karna's story is fascinating in the way so many vows and curses and boons come together across time and space.

Sahasrakavaci of Treta Yuga was reborn in Dwapara Yuga with the last of his armour, as Karna. Nara and Narayana were reborn as Arjuna and Krishna respectively to fulfil what had been set in motion in an earlier yuga—the pending final one-to-one battle with Sahasrakavaci.

Since it would take a thousand years of battle to rend Sahasrakavaci's armour as per Surya's boon, and Arjuna did not have that kind of time at his disposal, he used strategy to make Karna give away his magical armour in charity. Indra, who came disguised as a Brahmin mendicant to Karna, had asked for and received Karna's magical kavaca kundala in the form of alms, thus rendering him an ordinary human being.

Since it was now the turn of Nara to face Sahasrakavaci, Nara, as Arjuna fought the battle while Narayana, in the form of Krishna, supported him as his charioteer. The Kurukshetra war is where Sahasrakavaci met his end in his new life as Karna. And it took all the effort of the gods to finally achieve this.

Part II

Narayana-The Upholder of Dharma

chapter 1

Kamsa's Story

The story of Kamsa goes back to another time, another birth, when he was Kalanemi the demon. When Kalanemi's wife became pregnant, he was unaware that she was bearing *shadgarbhas*—six children in her womb: Hamsa, Suvikratu, Kratha, Damana, Ripumardana and Krodhahanta. The six foetuses began praying to Lord Brahma with such intensity that Brahma appeared, saying he would grant them what they wanted. The six foetuses wanted the boon of immortality, but they knew Brahma would never grant it. So they worded their request carefully: 'O Lord, grant us the boon that no one except our father be capable of killing us. Let no sage be able to curse us in any way.' Brahma had to grant the boon.

But once this boon was granted, it became necessary to stop the birth of the six demon foetuses. Since only their father could kill them, it became mandatory that such a situation be created. It required some strategy. So Sage Narada went to Hiranyakashyapa, who was the grandfather of Kalanemi and related what the foetuses had done in his inimical style. 'Narayana, Narayana, oops, I'm sorry, it has become such a habit that I am unable to rid myself of it. Anyway you know me well, I am impartial and I love to help people, especially the Asuras as they always get a raw deal.'

Hiranyakashyapa's visage changed from irritation to suspicion to pleasantness. When he heard from Narada of the boons gained by his yet-unborn great-grandchildren, he was furious. How dare the foetuses pray to Brahma for protection when he, their great-grandfather was still alive? Did they think he was unable to protect his own great-grandchildren? How dare the yet-unborn insult him—the great Hiranyakashyapa—whom all the people, be they devas, gandharvas, yakshas and asuras, trembled to behold? And beset with fury at the imagined insult, Hiranyakashyapa uttered a terrible curse, 'You do not deserve to live. May your own father kill you!'

Thus Vishnu ensured that in spite of the boon from Brahma, the lives of the six offsprings of Kalanemi would end. The next step was to prevent the birth of the shadgarbhas as Kalanemi's offsprings and have them reborn into a new life, so that their father could kill them. So Vishnu ensured that Kalanemi's wife had a miscarriage and the shadgarbhas were not born. Now the six of them had to be born elsewhere so that they could be killed by their father as per Hiranyakashyapa's curse. So Vishnu instructed Yogamaya to place the shadgarbhas into the womb of Devaki, one by one. The six children of Kalanemi of a previous birth, were born to Devaki successively, and instantaneously killed by Kamsa who was their father

Kalanemi, reborn. Thus the curse of Hiranyakashyapa was lived out from one birth to the other.

The demon Kalanemi had been killed by Vishnu. However, Kalanemi's balance sheet of sins and good deeds had not been evened out at his death. So Kalanemi was born as Kamsa to King Ugrasena of the Yadava dynasty. In his new birth, Kamsa was a dutiful son to his parents and a loving brother to Devaki initially. After the marriage of Devaki with Vasudeva, when Kamsa was personally escorting the newly married couple, a heavenly voice proclaimed: 'Kamsa, O foolish one, are you aware of what you are doing? You are taking death home! Devaki's eighth son will be the cause of your death.' The devilish streak of Kalanemi within Kamsa was stoked, and overcome with anger and fear, he dragged down Devaki from the chariot, and raised his sword to kill her. Vasudeva fell at Kamsa's feet and said, 'Mighty Kamsa! You who are so well-known for your valour, how can you stoop to kill a woman? Moreover she is your dear sister. I understand your fears and will hand over to you every child that is born of us so that you can ensure that you live a long life. Pray, do not kill your own sister and commit such a terrible sin.'

Kamsa was mollified and decided to keep the couple in his palace so that he could keep a constant watch on them. Sometime later Sage Narada visited him. Kamsa welcomed him warmly, 'O Great Sage, devotee of Maha Vishnu, your mere presence brings luck to those you favour. Pray, tell me how I may serve you.'

Sage Narada smiled and said 'Kamsa, you are a mighty

king. I want to remind you of your earlier birth. In your last birth you were known as Kalanemi. You were killed by Vishnu. However you are lucky to be born again. But you are not the real son of King Ugrasena.' Upon Kamsa's request Narada went on to reveal what nobody knew. Kamsa's mother Padmavati was a very beautiful woman and once when she was at the house of her father Satyaketu, a demonic messenger of Kubera called Drumila, saw her and was attracted to her. He disguised himself as Ugrasena and entered her chamber. Padmavati willingly gave herself up to what she considered to be her husband but during lovemaking, Drumila lost self-control and resumed his actual form. However, in the heat of the moment, Padmavati didn't protest and allowed herself to become impregnated by Drumila. Padmavati thus gave birth to a demonic son, Kamsa.

Hearing this, Kamsa's nature underwent a sudden and drastic change and the dormant demonic characteristics came to the fore. He remembered the divine proclamation that Devaki's eighth son would kill him and he ordered that Devaki and her husband be shackled and thrown into prison. In no time Kamsa turned into a tyrant. After the eighth-born of Devaki escaped from his clutches, Kamsa spent the next fifteen years of his life planning to kill Krishna. He was able to recall associate demons from his earlier birth and sent several of them to kill Krishna but Krishna slew them all. Finally Krishna came to Mathura, a fierce fight ensued between uncle and nephew, and Kamsa was killed, ridding the earth of an evil son.

chapter 2

The Chosen Couple—Devaki and Vasudeva

Towards the end of the Treta Yuga, there came a series of kings who were not great, and slowly good, wise governance was replaced with vice and war, and evil began to sprout in the Dwapara Yuga. For the reestablishment of Dharma in the new yuga, a new incarnation was needed. Mother Earth who had silently borne the brunt of the wicked, approached Brahma in the form of a cow. Seeing her tears, Brahma was moved. Even before she could relate her tale of woe, Brahma advised her to approach Narayana as he is the Protector of all, and had the power to help her.

Mother Earth went to Vaikuntha where Narayana rested on a couch made by the mighty snake Adishesha, amidst the milky ocean. Seeing Mother Earth in the form of a cow with tears streaming down her eyes, Goddess Lakshmi addressed her consort Narayana, thus: 'O Lord, Protector of all! My sister is here and she is in a pitieous state. There is nothing unknown to you. Is there a need for her to narrate her troubles? Please help her.'

Narayana raised his hand and smiled knowingly. 'Bhoomi Devi, your difficulties will soon come to an end. I will myself come forth as an incarnation. I will come as a child to Vasudeva and Devaki who themselves will be born because of a curse; and for the fulfillment of this curse, they will have to take birth. The Devas will come with me as my friends and remain there as long as I remain on earth. You may go and await my arrival.'

Hearing the promise of incarnation, Bhoomidevi returned, assured of the destruction of evil and the re-establishment of good.

~

Sage Kasyapa and his wife Aditi were to be born as Vasudeva and Devaki. Let us go back in time to see why they had to be born again.

Aeons back, Sage Kasyapa, a manasaputra of Brahma, had two wives—Aditi and Diti. Aditi was the mother of Indra and the Devas, and Diti was the mother of the Asuras. Once Diti, seeing the glowing Indra, approached her husband and begged him to give her a son, strong and powerful like Indra. Kasyapa granted her wish and soon she was heavy with child. When Diti was in her nineth month and the foetus was fully developed, Aditi, in a fit of jealousy, asked her son Indra to destroy Diti's unborn child. Aditi poisoned Indra's mind saying that the child, if born, would pose a great threat to him. Obeying his mother's command, Indra changed his form, entered Diti's womb and cut the foetus into seven parts and killed it. When Diti realized what had happened, she cursed Aditi thus: 'You are like a sister to me. We share the same husband. You have so many powerful and immortal children like Indra. Yet you have destroyed my child and caused me grievous hurt. You shall suffer the same. May you lose seven children. May you grieve over their deaths and suffer in a prison. May you spend a lifetime in sorrow.'

Aditi had to be reborn to live out the consequences of her action and Diti's curse. She was born as Devaki who had to suffer the deaths of seven children, one each for the seven parts the foetus had been cut into.

When Sage Kasyapa came to know of Indra's deed, he revived the seven parts of the foetus but they could not take human form. They became the seven *marut* or winds—Anaha, Vivaha, Samvaha, Ativaha, Anuvaaha, Parivaaha, and Vaaha who later became the associates of Indra at the request of Diti

Sage Kasyapa had earlier taken Kamadhenu—the holy cow—from Varuna to obtain offerings for his rituals and sacrifices. Several years passed and Sage Kasyapa, completely immersed in sacred rituals and holy austerities, forgot that he had to return Kamadhenu to Varuna. After waiting for a long time, Varuna asked Kasyapa to return Kamadhenu to him but Kasyapa gave excuses each time to Varuna, requesting to keep Kamadhenu for some more time. Finally, Varuna approached Brahma and sought his intervention. Seeing the covetousness of Kasyapa, Brahma was enraged and cursed

Kasyapa thus: 'You are a sage and should follow the path of righteousness. Instead, you are behaving in a selfish, covetous manner unbefitting of an evolved soul. Because of your greed to keep the cow, I curse you that you will be born as a mortal. Your wives Diti and Aditi will follow you in your next life. Aditi will suffer with you due to her karma, while Diti will lead a peaceful life in spite of being your wife.'

Thus Sage Kasyapa was reborn as Vasudeva into the Yadu clan, as the son of Shurasena. Aditi was born as Devaki and the two of them spent a large part of their lives as prisoners of Kamsa. Diti, on the other hand, was born as Rohini, the second wife of Vasudeva and though she lived away from her husband, she was happy with her son Balarama.

It was time for Devaki to bear her next child. In the meantime the gods, tired of Kamsa's mayhem, approached Vishnu and reminded him of his promise to redeem them from the atrocities of Kamsa. Vishnu pulled out two hairs from his head. One was white and the other black. Vishnu instructed Yogamaya to place these hairs into Devaki's womb one after the other as the seventh and eighth offspring of Devaki. Once the seventh foetus was fully developed, Yogamaya transferred it into Rohini's womb. Rohini gave birth to Balarama. Kamsa was given to understand that Devaki had suffered a miscarriage. As it was Vishnu's white hair of which Balarama was born, he was fair complexioned. Then for the last and eighth child, the black hair of Vishnu was placed in Devaki's womb. So was Krishna, or the Dark One, born.

Before the birth of Krishna, Vishnu appeared before the couple in his divine four-armed form bearing discus, conch, lotus and mace. They were overwhelmed. Having made them aware of the future, Vishnu entered the womb of Devaki. Thus Vishnu came to be incarnated and born as Krishna. Despite Vishnu's assurances, Vasudeva, fearing the death of his child, took the baby to his brother Nanda's home and exchanged it for the girl born of Yashoda, Nanda's wife. Miraculously the guards fell asleep, the prison doors opened, and Vasudeva's shackles broke loose when he had to take baby Krishna to Gokula. The waters of Yamuna also gave way for Vasudeva to cross, though it was in spate. Kamsa, when informed of the birth of the eighth child, came to the prison to kill it. When he threw the baby, which Vasudeva had brought from Nanda's home, against the wall, the infant vanished and there was a prophecy that the eighth child, who would be his death, was safe elsewhere.

Though Kamsa began searching for the baby who was destined to kill him and ordered his soldiers to slaughter all babies in his kingdom, he could not harm Vishnu who had been born as Krishna. And Kamsa did meet his death at the hands of Krishna later, thus fulfilling the curse.

chapter 3

Yashoda and Krishna

Krishna, the divine child, grew up in Gokula, giving joy to one and all, bewitching everyone with his beauty and charming pranks. Nanda's family priest Garga came and secretly performed the *namakarana,* or naming ceremony, for the two children together. Rohini's son was named Balarama and Yashoda's son was called Krishna.

Nanda, the Yadava cowherd chief and his wife Yashoda became the fortunate parents of Krishna, and Krishna grew up as a cowherd though he was of royal descent. Thus Yashoda enjoyed the antics of the Supreme God himself in the form of baby Krishna and Devaki spent her time in the prison bereft of all joy and happiness of a mother. The only solace that Devaki had was that one of her children was still alive.

Rohini, Vasudeva's second wife, was in Gokula and began living with Nanda and Yashoda. Rohini's son Balarama and Krishna were brothers by blood and grew up together as the best of friends.

As a small child, Balarama once caught Krishna eating mud. Balarama immediately went to Yashoda and reported Krishna's action to her. Yashoda came out and catching Krishna by his arm, asked him to open his mouth and show her what he was eating. Krishna shook his head and tried to free himself from her grip but Yashoda held fast. Finally, Krishna opened his mouth and lo and behold, the entire universe was visible in it. Yashoda lost her consciousness. When she recovered, she did not remember why she was there and went back to her house. Krishna had enlightened her but at the same time made her forget that he was god because with such a realization, Yashoda could never have brought up Krishna as her child.

As a small child, Krishna liberated two sons of Kubera who had been cursed by Narada.

Nalakubara and Manigriva were the sons of Kubera. Once they were playing in the waters of the Ganga with celestial maidens when Narada chanced on them while returning from a visit to Vaikuntha, the abode of Vishnu. The ladies immediately covered themselves but the two brothers remained blissfully unaware of the sage's presence. Pitying them for wasting their lives, Narada cursed them to be born as trees and await salvation upon Vishnu's touch.

One day, tired of his pranks, Yashoda tied Krishna to a grinding stone and went to fetch water. But the divine child crawled with the grindstone tied to him till it got stuck between two trees that grew close together. As Krishna tugged at the stuck grindstone, the two trees came toppling over, releasing the two yakshas who paid him obeisance and disappeared. Vishnu, in his birth as Krishna, had touched the cursed sons of Kubera and released them of Narada's curse.

When Krishna was still a child, Nanda and other elders of the village decided to migrate to Brindavana on the banks of the Yamuna. In Brindavana the grass was aplenty and the cows nurtured by Krishna and other cowherds produced milk in abundant quantities. But in the Yamuna lived the serpent Kaliya who was feared by one and all. Kaliya had made the river water inaccessible to the people. Krishna jumped into the river, fought with the serpent, tamed it and came out dancing on the hood of Kaliya. In return for sparing its life, Kaliya and his family of serpents left the river abode forever, thus freeing the waters of Yamuna for all.

Krishna not only freed demons from their existing forms and helped them attain salvation, but he also showed the world that arrogance, pride and other vices could ruin even gods and they too needed his divine grace to overcome these bad qualities. Once Brahma, forgetting that Krishna was Vishnu himself, assumed Krishna's tricks to be a manifestation of some magic. To test Krishna's power, he kidnapped his friends and took them away. A year later when Brahma chanced upon Krishna, he saw that all his friends were with him playing as usual. Brahma went to the cave where he had kept Krishna's friends and found that they were still there. Brahma was confused. It took him some time to realize that when he had kidnapped the boys, Krishna had created them again with his power so that mothers would not mourn the loss of their children who had actually disappeared. These forms were playing and doing exactly what the boys would have been doing in Brindavan. Krishna then transformed all the captive boys in the cave into the various forms of Vishnu, Siva and demigods. These forms sang the many names of god and danced.

When Brahma saw this he realized that Krishna was an incarnation of Vishnu. Brahma begged for forgiveness, offered prayers and penance for his action, and having circumambulated Krishna three times, returned to his heavenly abode.

Krishna had also taught Indra a lesson. Once when there was a long dry spell in Brindavana, Krishna convinced the people to pray to Govardhan hill instead of Indra. This infuriated Indra and he brought about unyielding rains, flooding Brindavana. Krishna provided a canopy of protection for all the villagers including their cattle by lifting the hillock Govardhan with only his little finger. Indra, not to be outdone, rained thunder and lightning and tried to destroy the hillock. After seven days of inexorable rain, Indra understood that the person he was fighting against was no ordinary child but Vishnu himself. Indra's arrogance was destroyed and he began performing his duties as ordained by the *Trimurthis* or 'trinity'.

Thus Krishna gave *moksha* to several beings, be they his devotees or demons or gods.

chapter 4

Salvation for Demons and Demonesses

King Kamsa was desperate to find Krishna and he sent evil beings in search of him. The first to be sent by Kamsa was Pootana, a woman with immense powers.

Pootana was Ratnamala, King Bali's daughter in her previous birth. When Vishnu had appeared at the court of King Bali in his Vamana avatar, Ratnamala was filled with a rush of great maternal instinct and she yearned to hold the boy to her breast and nurture him. Sensing her longing, Vishnu had granted her a boon to fulfil this wish. However, once Bali was pressed under Vishnu's foot into the *Patala loka*, Ratnamala, overcome with rage and grief, wanted to kill the boy who had caused it. Vishnu had granted her this wish also. In the great cycle of karma and rebirth, Ratnamala was reborn as Pootana.

In this life, Pootana was Kamsa's maid. She came in the form of a bird to Gokula and changed herself into a beautiful young lady. When she saw Krishna, milk flowed in her breasts. She entered Yashoda's home and got familiar with them. Yashoda was playing with Krishna and Pootana approached her smiling, 'Your child is so beautiful. Can I hold it for a moment and play with it?' Yashoda gave the child to her, unaware of her real nature. Pootana began playing with the baby and soon, when Yashoda became engaged with her household tasks, Pootana tried to feed him her breastmilk which was poisonous. According to Vishnu's boon to Ratnamala, Pootana thus had the opportunity to kill Krishna, who was actually Vishnu, by giving the infant poisoned breastmilk to suckle—and this action also fulfilled the boon that she would be able to clasp the boy to her breast and nurture him.

But Krishna was no ordinary child and he began sucking the life out of her. Pootana could not hold on to her human form anymore and the huge demoness fell dead while the infant Krishna played, seemingly unaware of what had happened. He had set Ratnamala free from the cycle of birth.

Once upon a time long ago there was a very troublesome son of Hiranyaksha called Utkacha, who regularly disturbed the sages in performing austerities. On one such occasion, Sage Lomasha was so furious that he cursed Utkacha, saying, 'May you lose the physical body with which you disturb sages, and become body-less.'

To his horror, Utkacha saw his physical body fall off like the skin shed by a snake. He fell at the sage's feet and begged forgiveness. But a curse once uttered, cannot be taken back. Sage Lomasha, touched by the plight of Utkacha and his genuine penitence, thought of a way of salvation from the curse. He gave a boon, 'When the feet of Vishnu touches you, you will be released from all your sins and attain moksha or salvation'.

Utkacha humbly asked, 'How will I reach Lord Vishnu's feet that I may be liberated from this curse? That in itself is a near impossible task.'

Using his yogic powers, Sage Lomasha said, 'It cannot happen in this life. You will take birth as an Asura. In that life, when you try to kill a baby, you will find salvation.'

Utkacha did not understand the logic of this boon, but humbly accepted it, knowing that the sage could see greater patterns than what ordinary people like him could. He would wait for another birth as was ordained.

Utkacha was born as Shakatasura and was in the court of King Kamsa. When Kamsa ordered him to find and finish Krishna, Shakatasura assumed the form of a cart and came over to Yashoda. Unwittingly, Yashoda placed baby Krishna in the path of the cart. Shakatasura was about to roll over the baby when Krishna kicked it with his tiny feet. In an instant the cart was broken into a thousand pieces and Shakatasura attained freedom from his demonic form.

Sage Lomasha's curse had been fulfilled and Utkacha was freed from his past sins.

Ages ago, there was a king called Sahasraksha. One day he was frolicking in the river with his wives when the irascible Sage Durvasa happened to come by, but the king ignored him, engrossed as he was with his companions. When Sahasraksha did not stop his consorting and pay due respect to him as was custom, Sage Durvasa took this as a direct affront and seethed inwardly, waiting. Then he raised his voice, 'You, Sahasraksha! It appears that you have forgotten your duties as a ruler. I curse that in your next birth you will be born a demon!'

Sahasraksha's wife who heard this, immediately warned her husband of the calamity that had befallen him. King Sahasraksha came to his senses and rushed out of the water to fall at the sage's feet, begging for forgiveness. Seeing the repentant king lying prostrate at his feet in penitence and humility, Sage Durvasa calmed down. He relented and blessed Sahasraksha with a boon—that he would attain redemption through Vishnu.

King Sahasraksha, in a later birth, was thus born as Trinavarta, or the tornado demon. He was one of Kamsa's allies. His unprecedented power to create whirlwinds causing mass destruction made him a fearsome evil force. Trinavarta was also sent by Kamsa to find and kill Krishna. Krishna was playing by himself when Trinavarta appeared. He grabbed baby Krishna and taking the form of a whirlwind, carried him away, intending to dash the baby to the ground and kill it. As Trinavarta rose into the sky, the child became heavier and heavier and Trinavarta found it increasingly difficult to move up. He decided to drop the child. In the meantime the child caught the demon's neck tightly and choked him to death. The *gopis* who had come in search of Krishna saw him playing on the chest of a dead demon. Sahasraksha had thus attained salvation at the hands of Vishnu as had been ordained by Sage Durvasa.

Krishna destroyed several other demons sent by Kamsa to kill him. Notable among them were Keshi, Kamsa's brother, in the form of a horse, who in his past birth was the demon Hayagriva; and Aristha who was Bali's son in his earlier birth and assumed the form of a bull.

In this manner many demons were freed of their demonic existence by the grace of Vishnu, in the form of Krishna.

chapter 5

Kamsa Meets His End

Kamsa, realizing that all his attempts to kill Krishna had failed, decided that he needed to kill Krishna himself instead of relying on his cronies. He decided to invite Krishna to his capital Mathura, and made plans of slaying him on arrival. Kamsa sent Akrura, a Yadava chief, to Brindavana to bring the two brothers Krishna and Balarama, saying that they would be feted for their exploits, news of which had reached far and near. Akrura was a devotee of Vishnu and hence of Krishna, and knew of Kamsa's plans. However, Akrura was bound by Kamsa's orders and had to follow them. Krishna and Balarama had also been waiting for the opportunity to destroy Kamsa and free their parents, Vasudeva and Devaki, from prison. This seemed a golden opportunity and they agreed to accompany Akrura.

Yashoda and Nanda did their best to stop Krishna from leaving and they were supported by all the villagers, the gopis and Krishna's friends. All had realized that Krishna would never return and they could not bear the thought of separation from him. However, Krishna too was bound to be led by fate which beckoned him to Mathura. Krishna and Balarama alighted at the gate of the Mathura palace. A huge elephant stood there seemingly to welcome them with garlands. But the elephant Kuvalayapeeda was a rogue kept by Kamsa. The elephant was Diti's son Dishta in its previous birth. It tried to trample Krishna and Balarama but Krishna jumped on its forehead and with one blow, killed it. Dishta was thus freed of his elephant birth.

Finally, Kamsa was left with no other option but to fight Krishna himself. He tried to put up a fight but it did not take much effort for Krishna to kill him. Then Krishna went to the prison and freed his parents. The meeting of Vasudeva and Devaki with their long lost sons was an emotional moment. Vasudeva and Devaki were filled with awe and reverence and it took some time for them to embrace Krishna as their son. Krishna also freed Ugrasena from the dungeon in which he had been held captive by Kamsa and installed him on the throne.

Thus was evil defeated and the rule of good established once more on earth—just as Vishnu had promised Bhoomidevi long back.

Part III
The Stage Is Set

chapter I

Yudhisthira—Dharma on Earth

Sage Marici was the manasaputra of Brahma. His son Sage Kasyapa married Aditi who bore him the Sun god Surya, or Vivasvan. Vivasvan rides through the skies covering the earth once every day in a chariot drawn by seven horses which represent seven days of the week. Surya was endowed with handsome looks, a well-sculpted body and more than anything else, a brilliance that helped him overshadow his rivals. One day he chanced on Princess Samjnaa as she stood on the terrace of her father's palace drying her hair. Princess Samjnaa was the daughter of Vishwakarma, the architect of the Devas. Surya nearly stopped his chariot but remembered his duty just in time and continued on his way. Later he sent his emissary to Vishwakarma with a proposal to wed his daughter.

Vishwakarma sent for his daughter. 'My dearest daughter, the gods have heard my prayers and sent you an eligible suitor. Surya has expressed a desire to have you as his consort. What shall I convey to his messenger?' Samjnaa bowed her head, blushing furiously. She had been thinking of Surya since she had seen him the previous dawn. She nodded ever so slightly and left the room immediately. Vishwakarma smiled knowingly and dispatched the messenger with an affirmative letter and gifts as was the custom in those days. The wedding of Surya and Samjnaa was performed with great pomp and show. They spent several years in perfect harmony and bliss. Samjnaa bore three children—Vaivasvata Manu, and the twins Yama and Yami also called Yamunaa. As the years passed, Samjnaa found Surya's heat difficult to bear. She expressed her feelings several times directly to Surya but he did nothing to alleviate her concerns. Once when she went to Vishwakarma's palace, he was surprised to see her looking wan and pale. 'My dear Samjnaa! Why do you look so weak? Are you not keeping well? What is the matter? You have become dark,' said Vishwakarma. Samjnaa broke into tears and wept her heart out. Vishwakarma met Surya and advised him to take care of Samjnaa. Surya was duly chastised and reduced his heat. As time flew by, Surya forgot Vishwakarma's advice and his luminosity began to hurt Samjnaa again.

Samjnaa began to spend less and less time with Surya and her children. She would wander off and return home after several days of solitude. Surya did not have time to observe her changing behavior. One day Samjnaa turned to see a mirror image of herself following her. 'Who are you? You look just like me! Why are you following me?' The mirror image replied, 'I am Chaayaa, your shadow. I belong to you, you are my mistress. I will follow you and do whatever you command me.' Samjnaa looked at her for a few minutes and then suddenly understanding dawned on her. She said, 'Chaayaa, I need you to do as I say. I am unable to live with my husband Surya. I want you to take my place in his residence and live with him.'

Chaayaa was taken aback and objected. 'How can I cheat your husband by taking your place? What if he finds out? I think this is not the right thing to do.' Samjnaa continued as if she had not heard Chaayaa, 'Please don't tell anyone of this. This is my order. Leave now.' Chaayaa nodded and left the place. Samjnaa transformed herself into a mare and left the spot. When Chaayaa turned to have a backward glance, there was no one around.

Chaayaa took the place of Samjnaa and assumed the duties of a mother and wife. Surya did not notice any difference. Years passed and Chaayaa bore Surya three children—Saavarni Manu, Shani, or Saturn, and Tapatii. With the coming of her children, there came about a change in Chaayaa's behaviour towards the children of Samjnaa. She began differentiating between her children and Samjnaa's offsprings. She would berate Yama and Vaivasvata Manu. She was particularly cruel to Yamunaa and would beat her often. Vaivasvata Manu suffered in silence; he did not utter a word against Chaayaa's ill-treatment of his siblings. He refused to join Yama when the latter went to their father to complain about his mother's behaviour. Surya listened to Yama's complaints with half an ear and always asked him to be more tolerant.

One day when Chaayaa hit Yamunaa, Yama was disgusted and approaching his father began rebuking him. 'You are not a good parent. Mother is beating Yamunaa and you don't bother to stop her. How can a mother be so cruel? I think she is not our mother. She is always nice to Saavarni Manu, Shani and Tapatii but is harsh on the three of us—Vaivasvata Manu, Yamunaa and me. She is a demoness in disguise. We want our mother, not this tormentor. If you do not do anything then we will leave the house immediately and will not stay with you and your wife.'

Surya was enraged and began beating Yama but Yama was belligerent and soon this led to a fight which brought Chaayaa there. Chaayaa screamed, 'Surya, you are his father! Stop please! Yama, stop this immediately or I will curse you.' Neither heeded her words. Chaayaa tried to separate them. Yama kicked her accidentally with his right foot.

Immediately Chaayaa cursed Yama, 'May you lose the use of your right leg! May it get infected with worms.'

Yama fell to the ground helpless. He turned to his father and said piteously, 'Do you believe me now? Can a mother be so pitiless that she would curse her own progeny? I admit that I kicked her in my rage but by her curse I have lost my leg forever.'

Surya bellowed, 'Samjnaa! What are you doing? Have you lost your mind? Retract your curse.' Chaayaa replied, 'I cannot and will not retract my curse. Yama has long troubled me and deserves this.'

'Samjnaa, you can't do this to your own son. What kind

of mother are you to cripple your own son?' said Surya.

Chaayaa lost control and shrieked out, 'I am not his mother and he is not my son. I am Chaayaa, Samjnaa's shadow. I came to live with you in her place because Samjnaa ordered me to do so. Samjnaa left you because she could not bear your glare. I have silently borne your radiance all these years.' Chaayaa fell to her knees and began weeping inconsolably.

Surya was lost for words. After a long spell of silence Surya said, 'Yama, my son, I cannot reverse Chaayaa's curse but I can reduce its effect. I will give you a rooster which will eat the worms in your foot and give you relief.'

He then turned to Chaayaa and asked her to relate everything—how she came to live with him. Chaayaa told Surya of her conversation with Samjnaa and the fact that she was only following her instructions.

Hearing all this, Yama was furious and began berating his father again. 'I told you she is not our mother. You are responsible for everything. Your inaction when I complained earlier has led to this situation. Now I have lost the use of my leg because of you and we don't know where our mother is. We have been suffering all these years due to your indulgence towards Chaayaa. You ignored your children for the sake of Chaayaa who was doing her wifely duties towards you. You must be punished for your irresponsibility. You must be answerable for your actions.'

Hearing his son accusing him, Surya's anger turned on Yama once more. 'You impudent boy! You know nothing about duties and obligations. Every action has a fruit attached to it.' And then Surya cursed Yama thus: 'You must learn how difficult it is to live a righteous life. May you be born on earth and live a mortal life where you will be called upon to think about every action and suffer its results.'

Yama was stupefied hearing his father's words. When Surya calmed down, he saw Yama's sorrowful face and said, 'My son, do not bewail your state. Every action has a meaning and a reason. It appears that the Trinity of Gods has a design, because of which these words came out as a curse. Go and pray to Siva. His blessings will help you.'

Surya went to Vishwakarma and learning that Samjnaa was in the form of a mare, became a stallion and wooed her. Samjnaa relented and she bore him sons—the Ashwini twins. Samjnaa then assumed her original form and returned with Surya to his abode. Chaayaa asked for forgiveness and Surya, on Samjnaa's insistence, gave her a place in their home and began living happily with both his wives. Vishwakarma chipped off some of Surya's effulgence and made him pleasant and bearable. The chippings of radiance were used to make weapons for the gods such as Vishnu's discus, Siva's trident and Indra's thunderbolt.

In the meanwhile, Yama performed severe penance and finally, Siva appeared before him. Siva said, 'I am pleased with your prayers and I am aware of your desires. I will give you responsibilities which will always highlight your importance in the world. You will be called Dharmaraja and it will be your responsibility to ensure that Dharma prevails in the world.

You will maintain records of the doings of all human beings and mete out suitable punishments or rewards to them after death. Remember, the soul of every human being will receive a new body based on his actions in the previous life. You will decide this for all the beings in the world. You, Yama, will be the God of Justice.'

Yama came to be prayed to by men with this hymn: *yamaaya dharmaraajaaya mrtyave caantakaaya ca / vaivasvataaya kaalaaya sarvabhuutaksayaaya ca:* salutation to yama, dharmaraja, death, terminator, son of vivasvan (sun god), time and destroyer of all beings.

And Yama came to be regarded as the lord of all our ancestors—*pitri*.

Ages passed thus till one day Kunti uttered a divine mantra and called on Dharmaraja Yama. The mantra was of such power that Dharmaraja Yama could not ignore the call and came down to earth. He blessed Kunti with a boon child, Yudhisthira.

This was the reason for Yudhisthira being considered an embodiment of Dharma or righteousness, and why everyone accepted his decisions as *vedavaakya*, or truth irrefutable. But as Yama's father Surya had cursed, making the right decision in difficult and ambiguous circumstances in accordance with the *shaastras* was no easy task. Hence Yudhisthira suffered the burden of his decisions, though he upheld all the rules and responsibilities and led a virtuous life. He especially upheld the most important Dharma of *satyam vada* 'speak the truth' and never spoke a lie during his entire life except on one occasion during the great war, when he uttered a half-truth. For this half-truth, Yudhisthira had to spend some time in hell.

It is important for each person to dwell on this. Every person deviates from the path of righteousness in his lifetime, and for all these sins big or small, he has to pay—either during his present life or in some future rebirth. And so are his good deeds harvested. The cycle of Karma continues inexorably, far beyond our understanding of Time and Space.

chapter 2

Bhima, the Brother of Hanuman

Sri Ramachandra, the hero of the epic Ramayana is considered to be an avatar of Vishnu. He came down to earth in human form in order to destroy the evil demon king Ravana, who had obtained a boon from Brahma—that he be immune to attacks from all beings except humans and monkeys. To aid Ramachandra, Brahma directed gods and goddesses to take birth on earth as *vanaras* or monkeys. Of them, Vali was born of Indra's powers, Sugriva from Surya, Nala from Viswakarma, the architect of the Gods, Gandhamadana from Kubera, Sushena from Varuna, Mainda-Dvivida from the Ashwini twins and Hanuman from Vayu.

Hanuman is present in both the great epics Ramayana and Mahabharata. When Ramachandra, pleased with Hanuman's love and selfless devotion, wished to grant him a boon, Hanuman requested for a sibling. He said, 'O Lord, I have witnessed the fondness that exists between you and Bharata. I have had no brothers or sisters. Grant me the boon that I may experience sibling love.'

Ramachandra replied, 'I am happy to grant your wish. However you will have to wait for another yuga. In the Dwapara Yuga, a son will be born to Vayu, who will thereby become your brother. This brother will be known for his strength and valour. He will learn from you your great virtues of steadfastness and humility. You will also help him in his war against the wicked.'

And so it happened that in Dwapara Yuga, the valiant Bhima was born of Vayu, to Kunti, when she used the mantra to call upon Vayu, the god of the winds. As prophesied by Ramachandra, Hanuman met his brother Bhima much later, during the period of exile of the Pandavas.

One day while Draupadi was resting and enjoying the cool breeze from the north, the divine scent of a flower wafted to her. After some time the breeze brought the dried flower to her and she was filled with longing for the fresh blossoms. Draupadi was living with Bhima at that time and requested him to get her the flowers. Bhima was eager to please his beautiful wife and set out following the scent wafting on the wind. Soon he approached a mountain and the path became narrow, wide enough only for one person to pass. There he found an old monkey with its tail lying across the narrow path. Bhima waited awhile hoping the monkey would go away for it was considered inauspicious to cross a supine person. After some time Bhima lost his patience and said, 'You are blocking my path. Move away. I am on an important mission.'

The monkey replied meekly, 'I am old and unable to

move. If you want to pass, you may lift me and lay me aside.' Bhima felt it below his dignity to obey a mere monkey, let alone pick it up in his arms, and showed his displeasure.

Seeing his reluctance the monkey continued, 'If you could move my tail aside that should clear your way.' Bhima decided to flick the tail away and move on. To his utter surprise, Bhima could not even move the tail, let alone flick it away. Then the ordeal began. Bhima tried to lift the tail first with one hand, with both hands and then with all the strength in his arms—but he simply could not move the tail!

It was then that Bhima realized this was no ordinary monkey but some divine being in the form of one. He was mortified about his arrogant attitude. Bhima prostrated himself before the monkey and said, 'O Great One! I beg your forgiveness for my haughty actions. Fool that I am, I did not recognize you. Please show me your true self!' In the twinkling of an eye, the old monkey disappeared and Hanuman stood before Bhima in all his glory.

This is how the boon that Hanuman would meet his brother and teach him humility, came true.

Hanuman embraced Bhima warmly and said, 'I have been waiting long to meet you, brother. What is it that brings you here?'

Then Bhima related everything to his divine brother Hanuman. He spoke of the treachery they had faced, of the Kauravas and their machinations resulting in their exile after the loss of their kingdom. Hanuman heard him out quietly till Bhima mentioned the flowers he had come in search of at Draupadi's request. 'I know where they bloom, brother,' said Hanuman and led Bhima to a nearby grove full of the beautiful blossoms. Bhima filled his arms with the blossoms, knowing how delighted Draupadi would be.

As time passed, Hanuman instructed Bhima in various techniques of battle, teaching him how best to use his phenomenal strength with strategy. It was clear to him that the prophecy was coming true—there was evil raising its head and taking control—something that would lead to a great battle between Good and Evil that he, Hanuman, was ordained to be a part of. Later, during the great war of Mahabharata at Kurukshetra, Hanuman positioned himself in the flag of Arjuna's chariot to secure and stabilize the warcraft. Arjuna, standing for Good, was thus aided not only by Krishna, but also by the power of Hanuman—both of whom were on his chariot all through the battle. The triangular saffron flag of Hanuman stands for stability and equilibrium, control of the senses and the mind. It also signifies the victory over all that is base and evil.

This is how a boon given by Ramachandra in another yuga came true and the brothers were united, and Hanuman played his part in the great battle of Kurukshetra.

chapter 3

Arjuna—Nara Reborn

Vali was born as a boon from Indra to Aruna, the charioteer of Surya. Aruna also begot another son from Surya, called Sugriva. Vali and Sugriva were kept in the care of Sage Gautama and his pious wife Ahalya. Anjanaa, the daughter of Gautama and Ahalya, communicated Indra's visit to the ashrama in Sage Gautama's absence. Hearing this, Gautama was enraged and turned Ahalya into stone. Ahalya, in turn, cursed Anjanaa to become a monkey. Hearing Ahalya curse Anjanaa thus, Sage Gautama turned Vali and Sugriva also into monkeys as they had failed to inform him about Indra's visit. Sage Gautama left the hermitage and went to the forests to perform penance. Before going, he left his three children in the care of Riksarajas, the king of Kishkindha.

After Riksarajas, Vali was crowned king of Kishkindha. Vali was extremely strong and had routed even Ravana who was renowned for his great physical strength. Vali had been blessed with a necklace given to him by his father

Indra. The wearer of the necklace would automatically be transferred with half the physical strength of his opponent in any battle. As such Vali was invincible. Vali and Sugriva lived in peace for a long time. Once a demon named Mayavi attacked Kishkindha. Vali fought with him and chased him away. When Mayavi began running away, Vali and Sugriva decided to pursue and kill him. Mayavi's trail led them to a cave. Vali entered the cave, while Sugriva waited for him at the entrance. Vali instructed Sugriva before leaving, 'I want to fight Mayavi on my own. Wait here for my return.' After several days of waiting, one day Sugriva heard loud animal sounds after which blood began flowing out of the cave. Fearing that Vali had been killed, Sugriva realized that he would not be able to finish Mayavi. So he rolled a huge boulder to the opening of the cave and sealed it completely. He thought that due to complete darkness, Mayavi would remain trapped in the cavern forever as he would be unable to determine the location of the opening to push the boulder away. Sugriva returned to Kishkindha and after a suitable mourning period, ascended the throne.

What had occurred was different. Vali had overpowered Mayavi and crushed him to death with his bare hands. The wild noises that Sugriva had heard were the cries of Mayavi during the throes of death. After the fight Vali realized that he was in total darkness and could not find the way out. After several months of captivity he was able to locate the entrance of the cave, dislodge the stone and emerge into light. He was enraged when he found out what had happened.

Though Sugriva surrendered the kingdom on Vali's arrival and pleaded forgiveness for what he had done in ignorance, Vali refused to forgive him. He banished Sugriva from his kingdom and forcibly usurped Ruma, his sister-in-law, much against the advice of his wife Tara. By committing incest, he sinned, and therefore was killed by Ramachandra.

When Sugriva left Kishkindha, Hanuman accompanied him though Vali beseeched Hanuman to remain with him. Hanuman knew that Sugriva was righteous and chose him over Vali. Sugriva and Hanuman took shelter on the peaks of Rishyamuka hill. Ramachandra and Lakshmana, while wandering in the forest in search of Sita, came to Rishyamuka hill. Rama and Sugriva became bound in friendship and each related his miseries to the other. Sugriva agreed to help Ramachandra in his search for Sita. In return, he asked Ramachandra to kill his brother Vali and crown him king.

Sugriva challenged Vali for a one to one combat. Since they were brothers and looked very similar to each other, Ramachandra could not identify who was who while they were fighting, and as a result, Sugriva suffered heavy injuries and accepted defeat. He asked Ramachandra, 'O Lord, why did you fail me? I confronted Vali with the belief that you would slay him with your arrows. I cannot face him alone due to the powerful necklace that he possesses. The moment I stand in front of Vali, he automatically gets empowered with half of my strength in addition to his own. That means, considering that we are equal, he becomes one and a half times stronger than me. How can I then win against him?'

Ramachandra said, 'I was unable to distinguish between the two of you and I did not want to kill you by mistake. Next time I shall not fail you. Challenge him again. This time wear a garland so that I know whom to shoot.'

Accordingly, Sugriva called Vali again to a duel the next day. Vali's wife Tara counselled him not to go for the duel a second time since she was suspicious about how Sugriva could return to fight so quickly after being defeated the previous day. But Vali did not listen to her advice and responded to Sugriva's challenge. This time Ramachandra did not let Sugriva down. His arrows unerringly found their target and Vali lay on the ground bleeding to death. Ramachandra approached him and Vali said, 'O Rama! You did not engage me in a combat, but aimed arrows at me standing behind cover. Is this the Kshatriya Dharma that you practice, for which you are well known?' Ramachandra explained gently, 'You banished Sugriva and took his wife. Sugriva sought my help to kill you. Since you are an animal, I am within the boundaries of Dharma in shooting at you from cover. Also, I need Sugriva's help to rescue my wife who has been abducted by Ravana.' Vali said, 'If only you had approached me. I have won against Ravana and he will do my bidding. I would have ordered him to return your wife and if he refused, I would have won her for you. Long ago, when Ravana challenged me, I tied him with my tail and spun him around the world before throwing him on the ground. I had Ravana imprisoned for several months. Finally, Ravana's mother approached me and fell at my feet, requesting me to release Ravana.' To this

Ramachandra replied, 'I know your strength but I cannot allow someone else to win my wife for me. That would be against my Kshatriya responsibilities.' Again and again, Vali accused him of having killed him in an unfair manner. Finally, Ramachandra said, 'I understand your feelings. You are born of Indra, and Sugriva of Surya. I have favoured Surya this time. In a next birth, I shall favour Indra against Surya so that you are vindicated. You, Vali, will get an opportunity to kill me from behind cover, just as I have done. No sin will be attributed to you for the act.'

True to this boon, in the Dwapara Yuga Ramachandra was born as Krishna, another avatara of Vishnu, and this was fulfilled. Krishna accepted death in the hands of a hunter, who was Vali reborn.

~

When Kunti uttered the mantra the third time and called upon the king of the gods, Indra, she was blessed with Arjuna. Nara was reborn as Arjuna to complete the last battle with Sahasrakavaci. Arjuna, the foremost of the Pandavas, was thus a part of Vishnu himself. Indra favoured Arjuna on many occasions and strengthened him.

chapter 4

The Ashwini Twins

Once upon a time there lived a king named Sharyati who was a wise and just ruler and people in his kingdom were happy and prosperous. He had a daughter called Sukanya, who had grown into a charming lady and several suitors sought her hand in marriage. She was known to be extremely beautiful.

One day, Sukanya went to her father the king and said, 'Father, I am tired of wandering in the palace gardens and staying inside the palace. I want to see the outside world. I wish to roam amidst nature freely. Please permit me to go out of the palace compound for some time. I promise to take care of myself. I only want to see the world of nature in all its pristine beauty and variety.' The King understood that Sukanya was feeling confined and would be unhappy if he took no action. So he ordered his soldiers to accompany his daughter and her attendants. 'Guard the princess; do not let her out of your sight even for a moment', was the king's order. Soon the princess and her companions enthusiastically set out for what seemed to them a great adventure.

In the forest bordering the kingdom lived several sages in their hermitages, where they performed austerities and penance. Sage Cyavana was one of them. He was the son of Sage Bhrigu, one of the manasaputras of Brahma and his wife Pulomi. Cyavana got this name since he was not born the normal way. When his mother Pulomi was pregnant, she was threatened by a demon. The demon carried her away on his horse. Pulomi was a brave lady. She jumped from the racing horse and somehow managed to reach the hermitage. However, while doing so, her womb was badly affected and the baby slipped out of the womb, falling to the ground. The baby was therefore named Cyavana, meaning the one who has slid down.

Such was the mystical power of the newborn that it stared at the demon pursuing his mother and the intensity of its look reduced the demon to ashes. Cyavana had saved his mother the moment he was born!

Cyavana grew up to become a mystic of immense powers, devout and erudite. He came to be known as Sage Cyavana and had been carrying out severe austerities for several years, sitting crosslegged under a tree in prayer, partaking neither food nor water. As the years passed while he sat thus motionless, his body came to be covered with anthills, till he appeared to be a large mound of earth. Only his eyes were visible through two holes, and they appeared to be like luminous balls.

Princess Sukanya and her companions, free of the confines of the palace, entered the forest and wandered about happily, plucking flowers and fruits, chasing butterflies and following songbirds. Soon it was dusk but they continued to ramble. After some time the princess, who was in the lead, failed to hear her companions requesting for rest, and was separated from them. She was chasing butterflies when she found herself in front of a mound with two glittering fireflies. She wanted to catch the glowing fireflies, so she took two twigs and thrust them into the two holes in an attempt to get them. 'Aaaaaaaaaaaaaaah!' A terrible scream pierced the forest. The princess was terrified. The cry had emanated from the mud heap! Sukanya turned back and ran for her life. Luckily she found her friends who were looking for her and together they returned to the palace.

The princess did not tell anyone about the incident in the forest. But she kept wondering about the shriek from the mound of earth. After they reached the palace, all those who had gone with the princess fell ill and experienced strange discomfort. The king was surprised at this turn of events and began making enquiries. Soon he learnt that the princess and her companions had been near the hermitage of Sage Cyavana. He realized that something had gone amiss. It was quite possible that someone from the group that had gone to the forest had disturbed the sage performing penance, and hence the distress caused to the sage was afflicting them all. He called everybody and asked them if anything unusual had happened during their time in the forest. Sukanya immediately knew that she was somehow responsible for what was happening. Her head hung in shame as she narrated how she had tried to catch fireflies with a stick and how a terrible scream had arisen from the anthill.

The king immediately rushed to the forest with his daughter. Indeed, it was sage Cyavana's ashrama and he saw a sage seated, withered with age and partially covered by anthills. The anthill on his face had fallen off and blood was flowing from his eyes. The king approached the sage with folded hands and appealed to him, 'O Divine Sage, I am King Sharyati and this is my daughter Sukanya. My daughter has committed a grave sin. She had come to the forest and mistaking your eyes for fireflies, she has unwittingly caused you blindness. I beseech you to bestow your forgiveness on her—she is innocent though her action has had a terrible consequence.'

When Sukanya saw the bleeding eyes of the sage she began trembling. She fell at his feet and cried out all that had happened. 'I only wanted to catch the fireflies, Sire. I did not know what I was doing. Please forgive me,' she sobbed.

Sage Cyavana said kindly, 'I know you did not do anything intentionally but I am now blinded. How shall I perform my daily rituals and ablutions?' He turned towards the king and said, 'O King, I seek justice. I know your daughter's action was out of curiosity and not malice. But I am helpless now as I am blind out of no fault or action of mine. Give me your daughter in marriage so that she can serve me.'

The king was shocked at the turn of events. How could

he give up his dear daughter to a life in the forest serving an old blind sage? All her desires, all her life would come to naught. The king was torn between duty and love and did not know what to say or do. In the meantime, princess Sukanya ordered for a holy fire to be brought. She then placed her hand over the fire and made a vow, ' I, Sukanya, take this vow, today, and at this moment, that I shall serve Sage Cyavana to the best of my abilities and till my last breath. I have taken away his eyesight and have meted out a punishment to him unknowingly. To pay for this sin, though it was unintentional, I shall marry him and take care of all his needs.' She then said to her father, 'Dear Father! I know you are in a dilemma. I wanted to relieve you from making a decision as I want you to be known as a just and fair ruler. I may be a princess but now I have committed a sin and must repent for it. Please arrange for my marriage to Sage Cyavana and bid me farewell. I shall live in the forest with him and assist him to perform all the rites. Do not grieve for me, Father. I am happy that my life has found a meaning and a purpose.' The king married off princess Sukanya to Sage Cyavana and the two left for the forest. Sukanya had cast off all her royal robes and jewellery and dressed like a sage's wife. Nobody who saw her now would know she was the princess of the land.

Several years passed. Sukanya served her husband with utmost love and devotion. She never felt sad or blamed her fate for having to leave the royal life and live in a hermitage. In fact she began to love her simple life in the forest.

One day, Sukanya was returning from a nearby rivulet

with a pot of water at her waist. Two handsome men, dressed in royal robes and adorned with the best of jewels came by her. They addressed her thus: 'Fair lady, what are you doing here in this forest? This is no place for a lady like you! You appear to be of royal descent yet you are dressed in ordinary clothes. Who are you?'

She was disturbed by their words but answered politely, 'I am Sukanya, wife of Sage Cyavana. We live in our hermitage nearby. I have come to take water for our daily needs from the rivulet that flows yonder.' So saying, she continued on her way. The men began following her saying, 'Devi, do not go away. You are so young and beautiful. We hear that Sage Cyavana is blind and old. Why do you waste your beauty and youth on him? What can an old hermit give you? You deserve to enjoy the pleasures of life. Come, choose one of us as your consort, and we shall fulfil your every desire.'

Sukanya was shocked. She turned to them angrily, 'How dare you speak to me in this manner? I am the chaste wife of Sage Cyavana. I love him and can never think about anyone else. If you speak another word in this vile manner I will curse you. Go away! Leave right now!' Sukanya continued towards her home but the two men accosted her still. She looked at them angrily and was about to utter a curse when the two men transformed themselves into their real form. She immediately recognized them as the Ashwini twins—Dasra and Nasatya. They raised their hands in blessing, saying, 'Devi Sukanya, we came here only to test you. We have seen your selfless service these many years. Ask of us a boon—whatever you wish we will grant you.'

Placing the pot aside, Sukanya prostrated before them in all humility. She raised herself and said, 'I have all that I can desire. I am happy with my life. I need no boon for myself. I request you to give my husband the boon of sight so that we can together perform our austerities. That is what I want most of all.' The Ashwini twins were pleased with her selfless request. They said, 'Sukanya, you are a great soul. You could have asked for anything for yourself but you have not been greedy or selfish. Instead, you have asked for the boon to be given to your husband so that his sight is restored. Because of this we shall grant him not only his sight but also his youth. Bring him here and we shall heal him. But you will have to pass another test before all this happens. You will have to recognize your husband once he is cured, from among the three of us.' Sukanya ran all the way to their ashrama and led Sage Cyavana to the Ashwini twins. They led Cyavana by hand to the rivulet as Sukanya waited on the bank. The three of them entered the water and immersed themselves completely. After a while as Sukanya stood praying, three identical men, young and handsome, came out of the rivulet. One of them spoke to Sukanya, 'Please identify your husband from among the three of us. Only then can you have him.' Sukanya looked at them but they looked the same and she took a few minutes to gather her wits. Then she prayed to Goddess Durga fervently for help. Goddess Durga directed her to choose the person whose eyes blinked, since only mortals blink. She then looked at the eyes of each of the three men intently. The eyelids of only one of them kept shutting and opening. The other two stared steadfastedly. Sukanya, flooded with relief, pointed out the one whose eyes blinked and without a shadow of doubt said, 'Here is my husband.'

The Ashwini twins took their original form and asked Sukanya, 'Is there any other boon you want?' Sukanya said 'Let the world benefit from your knowledge of healing and medicine. I request you to be born in the mortal world to spread your knowledge and teach people. This would help all on earth.' The Ashwini twins were once again impressed with Sukanya's noble and selfless nature and immediately accepted her request. Instead of giving Sukanya a second boon, the Ashwini twins would give the boon of medicinal knowledge to humankind.

Sukanya and her husband went to Sukanya's father, King Sharyati, took his blessings and returned to live in the forest peacefully.

∽

The Ashwini twins were born, as promised, several years later to Madri.

When Madri saw how Kunti could beget sons by the power of the boon given to her by the sage, she was consumed with the desire for motherhood. Madri could not stop herself and she went to Kunti, saying, 'I implore you to give me an opportunity to become a mother too. You know our husband cannot give us any children, but I long to be a mother, Kunti. I beg of you to allow me to use the mantra that you possess,' and Madri dissolved into tears holding Kunti's hands.

Kunti was deeply touched by Madri's plight and selfless as she was, Kunti gave her the mantra to use. She also advised Madri to use it immediately. Madri called upon the Ashwini twins, who appearing before her, granted her twins. It was the Ashwini twins who took birth on earth in order to fulfil the second boon Sukanya had asked for. In this new birth they were known as Nakula and Sahadeva, and they too played an important role in the Mahabharata.

chapter 5

Pandu's Story

Pandu did not want to ascend the throne of Hastinapur as he knew that his elder brother Dhritarashtra would become miserable. So on the pretext of enlarging the kingdom of Hastinapur, Pandu left with an army and spent many years waging wars. During the course of these conquests he acquired two wives, Kunti and Madri. After several years he returned to Hastinapur. The decision to replace Dhritarashtra with Pandu was yet in the discussion stage when Pandu went on a hunting expedition to the forest. There he saw a couple of deer engaged in sexual intercourse and without a second thought, shot the deer with arrows. With a terrible cry the deer fell down and to Pandu's amazement turned into a human couple!

The man bemoaned loudly, 'I am Sage Kindama by name. You have killed me when I was engaged in the act of love. How can a just king behave in this manner! I will therefore curse you.'

Pandu interrupted the sage and said, 'I am not to blame. How would I know that you are a sage and not an animal? I am a king and hunting is a pastime for a Kshatriya. No sin is attributable to killings during hunting, or war. I am just and you cannot curse me.'

Sage Kindama thought awhile and said, 'O king, I agree that you thought I was an animal. However, it was a beastly action to kill even an animal when it is in the throes of passion. Since you shot at me without realizing that I am human, you will not be touched by the sin of *Brahmahatya* (killing of a Brahmin). However, since you have killed me in my moment of ecstasy, I curse that you will lose your life when you become intimate with a woman. Also, you have killed my mate for no fault of hers. So the woman who becomes responsible for your death will also give up her life. May you suffer the same way as my mate and I have.'

So saying, the sage fell dead on the body of his prone wife who had already given up her life.

Pandu was very upset at this turn of events. The curse meant that he could not have conjugal relations with his wives. It also meant that he could not have sons to continue his line. Was this what Kunti and Madri deserved for having married him? Dhritarashtra was childless and all in the royal family had pinned their hopes on Pandu and his wives. Now, this curse had changed the entire situation. The guilt-ridden Pandu decided to embrace an ascetic's life and left the palace. Despite his attempts to dissuade Kunti and Madri from accompanying him, they rejected all his arguments and followed Pandu to the forest.

In the forest, Pandu was unable to concentrate on his duties and constantly worried about the fact that he would die without any progeny to take his name forward. The shastras say that there is no salvation for one without a son (*aputrasya gatir naasti*). He was also guilt ridden by the fact that his wives would have no one to take care of them in their old age. He repeatedly shared this grief with Kunti and began imploring her to practice the niyoga method to bear children and thereby take his line forward. However, Kunti was against using this method and consistently avoided Pandu's appeals. Finally, one day when Pandu exclaimed, '*Aputrasya grham shuunyam*', meaning, a childless home is emptiness indeed, Kunti broke down. It was time she told her husband of the boon she had received as a maiden, by which she could call upon any god to bless her with a son.

She began hesitantly, 'Dear husband, I beg you to forgive me. I have held on to a secret all these years without sharing it with you for fear that it will upset you. I beseech you to hear me out completely before saying anything or taking any decision.' Having received *abhaya pradaana* from Pandu—a blanket permission to say everything without fear—Kunti told him all about Sage Durvasa's boon with which she could get a son from any god she wished. The child that would be born thus would have the qualities of the god invoked. 'I can use this mantra four times', she said, 'and each child will have the qualities of the god he is born of. This would be an equivalent of the niyoga method with the added sanction of gods. The children obtained by this boon would have not mortal men, but gods as their fathers. If you permit me to use this boon, we can overcome the sorrow of not having offsprings to carry on the lineage.'

Kunti did not tell Pandu about her experiment with the mantra before her marriage and the son that she had had when she was still a virgin. She had never talked of it to anyone, burying the secret deep inside.

Pandu's delight knew no bounds. 'My dearest wife, your words are like nectar to me! Why did you delay telling me this for so long? Do you not know how much I trust you? Did you not have faith in me? Please do use the mantra and let us fulfil our married life with the coming of our descendants.' Pandu's pleasure delighted Kunti and she replied, 'I was a fool to fear your reaction. As my husband, it would be right for you to choose the god who should be the father. Please instruct me on whom to invoke by the power of the mantra.'

On Pandu's advice, Kunti appealed to three gods consecutively and obtained three sons—Yudhistira, Bhima and Arjuna respectively. Madri invoked the Ashwini Kumars and bore Nakula and Sahadeva—the twins. In no time Pandu's childless existence was filled with the laughter of five sons—the Pandavas as they came to be called.

Pandu continued to live happily in the jungle with his wives and children. They never thought of returning to Hastinapur since Pandu and his wives had already taken up the ascetic way of life. One day, when the children were about five years old, Kunti took all the five children with her to gather fruits and flowers from the forest, leaving Madri to take care of Pandu's needs. In her absence, Pandu was suddenly overcome with lust while looking at Madri—the woman he had found so attractive that he had married her at once during a conquest. All the years of celibacy and self control fell away as Pandu clasped Madri passionately to his chest and she melted in his arms with inflamed passion. Neither realized what they were doing till, in the throes of ultimate passion, Pandu fell off, dead. Despite all the sacrifices Pandu had made, the curse of the sage that he would meet his death in the throes of passion, had come true.

Cursing herself as the cause of Pandu's death, Madri jumped into Pandu's funeral pyre, leaving her twins in the care of Kunti. Thus Kunti was left to raise all the five Pandavas by herself.

chapter 6

Gandhari's Story

Gandhari was brought from her father's home to Hastinapur by Bhisma with great pomp and married to Dhritarashtra. She was the paragon of virtue and served her blind husband devotedly. But despite many years of marriage, she was unable to produce an heir to the throne. Gandhari was unable to conceive despite all her fasts and prayers.

Once when Sage Vedavyasa came to Hastinapur, Gandhari served him with great dedication as he was not only a great sage but also her father-in-law. Pleased with her sincerity and devoutness, Vedavyasa wanted to give her a boon. He asked her what she craved for most and Gandhari opened her heart out to him. 'O Great Sage! I arrived in this palace several years ago yet I have been unable to conceive. My husband is dissatisfied with me and seeks the company of other women and vindicates himself. When I arrived, Bhisma blessed me pronouncing '*shataputravatii bhava*' (may you be blessed with a hundred sons). Ever since that day I have seen myself as a mother to hundred sons. Please give me the boon to fulfil this. I shall be ever grateful to you. I know that with your austerities you have the power to grant me this boon.'

Vedavyasa uttered *tathaastu* (so be it). Shortly afterwards Gandhari became pregnant. She was the happiest person in the world. Dhritarashtra too began to treat her with affection as soon as he realized that she was carrying his progeny who would ascend the throne of Hastinapur since Pandu had been cursed and was living the life of a celibate in the forest.

But Fate took a different path of its own. Two years passed and yet Gandhari showed no signs of delivery. Medicines and prayers failed to produce results as the heavily pregnant Gandhari waited and waited for the birth of her child.

In the meantime news of the birth of Yudhisthira to Pandu from his wife Kunti, reached the palace. Dhritarashtra flew into a rage because his child had not yet come into the world and therefore, by the rule of primogeniture, the eldest son of Pandu would be the future heir to the throne. Dhritarashtra hated the very thought of the Pandavas coming to power. He berated Gandhari, blaming her for not giving birth and screaming curses at her, he stomped out of her chamber, ordering her to send her maid Sauvali to serve him instead.

Gandhari dressed her maid in all finery and sent Sauvali to appease Dhritarashtra's passion. After Sauvali left, Gandhari wept in sorrow and fury, and in a fit of rage at her inability to give birth, she began to rain blows on her stomach repeatedly with all her strength. As a result she went into labour. But the fruit of her pains was nothing human—it was a shapeless mass of flesh! When Satyavati, Ambika and Ambalika rushed in and saw what had happened, Satyavati realized the crisis was bigger than what they could handle. She called out to her son Vedavyasa, remembering his vow that he would come whenever she called for his help. Sage Vedavyasa appeared before her and consoled Gandhari, 'My daughter, do not weep. You should have had patience. What made you do this?' Gandhari fell at his feet and wailed, 'I had waited for two years, Sire, but when I heard of Kunti's fortune, I could not control myself anymore. She who was supposed to be childless, now has five sons while I, who was supposed to give an heir to the throne, has none!' Gandhari was beside herself with pain and grief. 'Please do something. You yourself have blessed me with a boon! You said I will have a hundred sons. Will that boon go in vain? Help me, O help me, Sire!'

Vedavyasa shut his eyes and kept silent for some time. Then he addressed Satyavati and asked for a hundred pots of clarified butter, or ghee. Then Sage Vedavyasa did the unthinkable—he cut up the lump of flesh that Gandhari had aborted, into a hundred pieces and put a piece of it in each of the hundred pots of ghee, covering them. However, there was still a small piece of flesh left. Gandhari saw it and said, 'O Great Sage, I do not know how to express my gratitude for having blessed me with a hundred sons. Now I wish I had a daughter also. Please grant me a girl too.' Vedavyasa got another pot of ghee and placing the last piece of flesh in it, uttered a stern warning. 'Gandhari, make no mistake this time. Do not open the jars before nine months. After the said period each pot will bear you a child and you will have 101 offsprings—a hundred sons and one daughter.' Saying this, Vedavyasa departed.

Gandhari patiently waited for nine months and then were born, one by one, a hundred sons and a daughter. All the children were of Kuru lineage, so they were referred to as the Kauravas. This time none of the ladies, Satyavati, Ambika or Ambalika, taunted Gandhari. Instead, they took great care of her. They had heard Sage Vedavyasa's words and knew these would not be ordinary children—born as they were out of pots instead of a mother's womb.

Duryodhana was the firstborn. As soon as he came into this world, he started braying in a strange manner, like a donkey. Immediately there were yelps and howls from all directions. Beasts from the forest made their presence felt. There were sinister omens of violence all around—jackals howled, fires raged, winds blew. It was a clear indication that Duryodhana's birth was not an auspicious one and all the learned elders headed by Vidura advised Dhritarashtra and Gandhari to dispose the baby without delay as he would bring only ill-luck and ruin to the kingdom. Vidura said, 'This son of yours brings hate and destruction with him into this world. He will destroy your lineage if you do not destroy him. Get rid of him now, else it will be too late.' He quoted a wise saying—*tyajed ekam kulasyaarthe*: a single entity may be abandoned for the sake of a family.

But Dhritarashtra and Gandhari were blinded by the joy of parenthood and refused to listen to the advice of Vidura and others. This was the second mistake committed by Gandhari, continuing the first one that had led to her delivering a lump of flesh instead of a child. It was also wrong of Dhritarashtra to neglect the advice and portents that clearly indicated something was amiss. These actions led to a chain of events whereby the attachment for the firstborn led them to commit grave injustices and they paid a heavy price in the end—the death of all their children. After Duryodhana, the other sons were born. The daughter born last was named Dusshala.

In the meantime, Gandhari's maid—the one she had sent to appease Dhritarashtra—gave birth to a son, Yuyutsu, who came into the world just after Duryodhana. But since Sauvali was not a Kshatriya woman, her son from Dhritarashtra remained a *daasi-putra*. He was never treated with respect by his brothers though he was second only to Duryodhana and was elder to the other ninety-nine brothers.

chapter 7

The Transformation of Shikhandi

Drupada was the king of Panchala kingdom. For a very long time he did not have any children. He longed for a son. He performed austerities in the forest with great devotion, and prayed to Siva fervently. Siva was pleased and appeared before him. 'Drupada, arise and ask for a boon', he said. 'I am happy to bless you. You have performed penance with great sincerity for a very long time.' An overjoyed Drupada stood with folded hands, saying, 'O Great Lord of the universe! There is nothing in this world that escapes your eye. I am a minion in your realm. You are aware of the desires that lie in the depths of my heart. Pray bless me. I am happy to receive whatever you give me.'

Siva smiled and said, 'By my boon, you will have a female offspring.' Drupada was crestfallen since he had expected the boon of a son to be the heir to the throne after him. He appealed to Siva, 'O Lord! Have pity on me. I have been wanting a son to continue my lineage but you have blessed me with a daughter. Please grant me a son.' Siva said, 'I cannot retract my boon. I have given this boon for a particular reason. The girl child has a purpose. However, since you request me, I will alter the boon a little. You will have the daughter but will bring her up like a son. She will in time to come be transformed into a man. In this manner my boon will not be retracted and your desire will also be fulfilled.' So saying, Siva vanished

Drupada was disappointed and confused but he had no choice. It was better than being childless, he thought, and he would bring up the girl child like a prince. In due course, Drupada's wife gave birth to a baby girl. Though Drupada was not happy since Siva had foretold that the girl would change into a boy, Drupada reared the baby as a boy and named him Shikhandi. He got her trained in the art of warfare and administration, just like a prince.

What nobody knew was the reason why Siva had given the boon of a girl child, and what was her purpose in this life. This child was princess Amba reborn in order to take her revenge. Since Amba had ended her life abruptly in her previous birth, she had to complete that period of her previous birth as a woman, as was ordained. Therefore, she had to be reborn as a girl. Before dying, Amba had got a boon that in her next birth she would be responsible for the death of Bhisma, and for that she needed to become a man. Siva, who could look into present, past and future, had thus foretold that she would be transformed into a man after the period of womanhood was completed.

When Shikhandi came of age, King Drupada got his offspring (in the guise of a boy) married to the daughter of Hiranyavarna, the king of Darshana. In the nuptial chamber when Hiranyavarna's daughter realized the deception, she ran out and poured out to her father her tale of woe. Hiranyavarna was furious that his daughter's life was destroyed, and immediately declared war on Panchala. This was a revelation to Shikhandi also, since Shikhandi had always believed himself to be a man as he had been brought up so. Suddenly Shikhandi lost his sense of self and identity. The shock was terrible. In order to avert the war, and deeply distressed, Shikhandi left the palace. Unable to accept that he was actually a girl, Shikhandi decided to fast to death.

But Fate had laid out a different trajectory for Shikhandi. A yaksha called Sthunakarna chanced upon Shikhandi, and hearing her tale of grief, offered to help her. The yaksha would use his magical powers to transfer his manhood to Shikhandi in exchange of hers, for a period of time. The plan was that Shikhandi would return to Panchala, fight Hiranyavarna, and having killed him, would return to Sthunakarna the manhood he had given Shikhandi. During that period, the yaksha would be a woman while Shikhandi became a man.

Shikhandi thus returned to Panchala as a man and fought with Hiranyavarna. Having killed Hiranyavarna, Shikhandi returned to the forest to exchange his gender with the yaksha again. But things were not the same as before. In the meanwhile Kubera, the master of all yakshas and yakshinis, had learnt of Sthunakarna's gender exchange. Since Sthunakarna had not sought Kubera's permission before taking such a drastic decision, Kubera was incensed. In a fit of rage Kubera cursed Sthunakarna that he would be unable to get back his gender until Shikhandi died a natural death.

When Shikhandi learnt what had happened to the yaksha who had so kindly helped him, he was deeply repentant and decided to do penance. When Shikhandi approached some sages for guidance, they told him about his previous birth as princess Amba, her abduction by Bhisma, her boon from Siva and her immolation. Shikhandi realized that he was destined to kill Bhisma and therefore all forces had come together to help him become a man so that he could achieve this end. Shikhandi also understood why he had to be born as a woman first and then be changed into a man.

After having learnt about his previous birth, Shikhandi returned to Panchala. At the palace gate he saw the garland of ever-fresh lotuses which had been thrown there by princess Amba. Shikhandi wore the garland and entered the palace. When Drupada saw Shikhandi, he was delighted that as per the boon of Siva, Shikhandi had become a man and his period of womanhood was forever over. Prince Shikhandi would be the heir to the throne of Panchala and carry on the lineage.

chapter 8

Nalayani's Five Boons and Draupadi

In the Treta Yuga there lived a beautiful and virtuous lady Nalayani, also called Indrasena. Her mother had passed away at her birth and for a few years she was brought up by her father. Her father then married again. Nalayani was ill-treated by her stepmother at every instance. Her stepmother hated her and after Nalayani's father's death she made Nalayani's life a living hell. When it was time for Nalayani's marriage, she was married off to an irascible leper—Sage Maudgalya. But Nalayani was not an ordinary woman. She served her husband and took care of all his needs. She would bathe him every morning and tend to his wounds. She would help him do his religious rituals, cook, serve him with devotion and then partake of what was leftover. Despite the fact that her husband was a leper, she never once desired another man, and was an embodiment of chastity. She never once complained to anyone about her piteous state.

One day, after her husband had finished his meal, she

sat down for her meal. In those days it was customary to eat out of the same banana leaf used as a plate by one's husband. Also, the custom was that the husband would deliberately leave some food for his wife's consumption. To her shock, Nalayani saw that her husband's thumb had fallen off onto the plate. She did not show any revulsion but served herself and completed her meal with equanimity, even eating the thumb as part of the leftovers. After finishing her meal she found that her husband was nowhere to be seen. She searched the hermitage but could not find him. Finally she went out and found him lying dead. She took the body in her arms and wailed out aloud. She beat her chest and cried at his death. She decided to do *sahagamana*—enter the funeral pyre with her husband's body and immolate herself. She bathed her husband for the last time and then having bathed herself, dressed up in all finery. Nalayani prepared the pyre and just as she was about to enter her husband's pyre, Siva appeared before her. He said, 'My child! I am pleased with your devotion to your husband. You have served your husband without desiring anything in return. You are truly a *pativrataa*. Ask what you want and you shall be granted that.'

She fell at Siva's feet and uttered '*patim dehi*' (Grant me a husband). Since Siva did not say anything, she repeated her request four more times. At last Siva said '*tathaastu*' (so be it), and disappeared. Nalayani understood that she would have to wait for another birth to fulfil the boon. She entered the pyre and gave up her life.

Now the woman had desired the pleasures of conjugal

life, but had uttered her request for a husband five times. When Siva granted that her desire would be fulfilled, the boon included all the five requests for husbands. In some birth she would live with five husbands simultaneously!

Why did Siva grant a boon that would mean having five husbands?

The story goes even further back in time and space, to fulfil a curse uttered by Brahma.

Once five goddesses—Shyamala, wife of Dharmaraja, Bharati, wife of Vayu, Sachi, wife of Indra, and the two wives of the Ashwini twins—had teased Brahma in jest. But, enraged by the jest, Brahma had cursed all of them to be born as mortals on earth. They fell at Brahma's feet and pleaded with him, 'O Venerable One! Have pity on us. We behaved with levity—and understand that it was wrong of us—but do we deserve such harsh punishment? We cannot live away from our husbands for a lifetime on the earth. Pray, retract your curse. Give us a solution or a way out!'

Brahma calmed down and after pausing awhile to reflect on the situation, said, 'Once uttered, my words cannot become false. The curse has to take its course. However, I can modify the curse a little so that its effect is reduced. You five ladies will share the same earthly body when you are born on earth. This would mean that you can live on the earth together, and for a shorter period of time—a single lifetime.'

The five goddesses came to reside in the physical body that Nalayani attained when she was reborn. Nalayani, in her next birth, was Draupadi.

Brahma's curse and Siva's boon aligned in the great scheme of things, giving Draupadi five husbands who were born of Dharma, Vayu, Indra, and the Ashwini Kumars—the five Pandavas.

Part IV
The Great Churning

chapter 1

Drona and Drupada

Drupada was the son of King Prishata of Panchala. He studied under the tutelage of Sage Bharadwaja. Drona was the son of Sage Bharadwaja and studied along with Drupada. They grew up together and became very good friends. As the years passed, the bond between Drupada and Drona grew deep and Drona never felt that Drupada was a prince and he a poor Brahmin's son. Once schooling was over, Drupada got ready to return to Panchala. Before leaving, he hugged Drona and made a vow. He promised that when he became king, he would share his kingdom with Drona. Neither thought that a day would come when this vow would be called to test.

After some time, Drona learnt that Sage Parashurama was giving away all his possessions. Since Bharadwaja was very poor, he advised Drona to seek Sage Parashurama for charity. Drona went to Sage Parashurama with great expectations but by the time he reached the hermitage, the sage had given away all that he had. Seeing Drona approach, Parashurama said, 'My son! I do not have anything left with me to give you. However, I still have my weapons. I can teach you their usage. I can also initiate you with divine mantras to use with the arrows.'

Drona became his pupil and received a vast storehouse of knowledge in the art of war. Drona learnt the usage of powerful weapons like the *Brahmastra*. With this knowledge Drona became an *acharya* or 'teacher' in warcraft. In a marked deviation from later times, and unlike Brahmins of those times, Drona, and Parashurama before him, took up weapons and became teachers of warfare instead of Vedic studies. But he remained poor.

Unable to make ends meet, Drona decided to approach his childhood friend Drupada, for help. Drona never expected Drupada to give him half the kingdom of Panchala as had been promised; he was only looking for some financial help from his friend. But Drupada, who had succeeded his father Prishata to the throne, was afraid that Drona would remind him of the childhood vow and stake claim to half the kingdom. To ward off such a possibility, Drupada went on the offensive and humiliated Drona saying that friendship was possible only between persons of equal stature. Drupada, a king, did not want to have anything to do with Drona, who was a poor teacher. Drupada's arrogance touched the limits when he said that he was willing to give Drona alms only if Drona begged him. Drona was shocked and furious by the way his friend had treated him and he silently left the palace. But in his heart Drona vowed to take revenge and teach Drupada the meaning of friendship. Drupada's arrogant rejection of an old friend sowed the seeds of what was to follow.

Drona became the guru of the Pandavas and Kauravas, training them in the art of warfare that he had learnt from the great Parashurama. The princes spent several years in learning the usage of different weapons, politics, war strategies, army management, etc. Each prince excelled in some particular weaponry. Yudhisthira chose the lance, Bhima and Duryodhana the mace, Arjuna the bow and arrow, and so on. During this period Duryodhana made several attempts to kill the Pandavas, especially Bhima. Notable among these endeavours was giving poisoned food to Bhima and his subsequent drowning in the river infested with poisonous snakes. This endeavour boomeranged as the poison of the snakes reacted with the poison in Bhima's stomach and therefore caused no harm. Additionally, in the riverbed Bhima met the King of Snakes, Adishesha, who blessed Bhima with the strength of ten thousand elephants.

After their training came to an end, the Kauravas and Pandavas approached Guru Drona and asked him how they could give *gurudakshina*. Drona said 'I have been waiting for this day since a very long time. I want you to fight King Drupada and bring him as a prisoner to me since he had insulted and humiliated me for being poor.'

Immediately Duryodhana sprang into action. He said, 'I will fight King Drupada and bring him. I have the mighty armies of Hastinapur at my disposal.' However Duryodhana was no match for King Drupada and he returned defeated.

Then Drona addressed Arjuna thus: 'My dear Arjuna, you have promised to give me what I asked for, at the beginning of your training. I have made you the best archer in all the land. Now you must repay me. Go and bring King Drupada to my feet.' Arjuna bowed, took Drona's blessings and headed to Panchala. Arjuna led the Pandavas against Drupada and won a decisive victory, capturing Panchala as well as King Drupada. They brought Drupada bound in ropes to their guru Drona. Drupada had lost all his arrogance and he stood bereft of all the trappings of royalty before the poor friend he had once so brazenly rejected.

Drona set Drupada free. He divided the kingdom of Panchala into southern and northern parts. Drona returned the southern part centered at Kampilya to Drupada and retained northern Panchala, centered at Ahichatra, and made his son Ashwathama its ruler. Then Drona embraced Drupada and sought to revive the friendship that had existed between them during their childhood. He said, 'Drupada, let us be friends again. You need not feel awkward to accept my friendship because both of us are equals now in wealth and power. Earlier you did not want the world to know about our closeness because I was a poor Brahmin. I made Arjuna win your kingdom and give it to me as gurudakshina so that I could return half of it to you, thus making us equals.'

Drupada had no option but to take a part of the kingdom that had been his. But his Kshatriya pride had turned to hatred and he seethed inwardly at the humiliation he had suffered. Drupada vowed to have his revenge and see Drona dead.

Though Drupada's own arrogance had set the chain of vengeful actions in motion, he never realized it and instead of correcting his course, he rushed headlong into more vengeance.

~

Drona and his son Ashwathama never ruled the kingdom they acquired. They remained at Hastinapur and became part of Dhritarashtra's court. Duryodhana patronized Ashwathama from the beginning, as he wanted to please Drona. Ashwathama was jealous of Arjuna as Arjuna was Drona's favourite pupil and had gained all the knowledge that his father had, some of which Drona had denied to teach even his own son. As Ashwathama was in Duryodhana's camp, Drona could never oppose Duryodhana against the atrocities he committed. Even during the Mahabharata war, Drona had to fight on the side of the Kauravas despite knowing that it was wrong, because Drona felt indebted to Dhritarashtra for having given him a means to livelihood when he was penniless.

Such is the way actions are linked in a chain, and nobody knows which cause may lead to which effect in time to come.

chapter 2

Karna and Duryodhana— an Unlikely Friendship

After the completion of the princes' education, an events display was held so that all the people of Hastinapur could view the skills that the princes had gained in the years spent with Dronacharya. Each of the princes displayed his prowess in a chosen weapon. Friendly duels were held between some and some gave solo performances. Bhima and Duryodhana fought a duel with maces which was a spectacle to be seen. From a *pratispardha* (display), it turned to a regular combat with each trying to kill the other. Noticing this development, Drona immediately asked the combat to be stopped.

After Arjuna's feats in archery, Drona proclaimed to all that Arjuna was the best archer in the entire kingdom. However, his assertion was cut short when a very confident archer appeared wearing glittering divine armour and earrings, and threw him a challenge. He said, 'I, Karna, would like to have a duel with you, Prince Arjuna. I can prove that

I am better than you. Come and face me.'

Drona immediately recognized Karna as the boy who had approached him with the request that he be taught the art of weaponry and warfare. But Drona had refused to be his guru because Karna was the son of a charioteer and hence had no right to learn the art of Kshatriyas. Drona watched with growing concern as Karna performed all the feats that Arjuna had demonstrated, and then challenged him to a duel.

Drona did not want the duel to happen, since traditionally, a duel should be between equals, and Karna, being a charioteer's son could not be considered equal to Arjuna who was a Kshatriya and a prince. So Drona ordered Arjuna to refrain, citing Karna's background. Seeing this, Duryodhana realized that a golden opportunity had presented itself to put down the Pandavas. Seeing a chance to make an ally and improve the strength of his side, Duryodhana decided to ignore the strict rules of caste. He rose from his seat and going into the arena, embraced Karna, declaring aloud, 'I hereby make Karna the king of Anga. Thus he becomes eligible to participate in this show of skills. Let there be a duel between him and Arjuna.' For Karna, who had faced discrimination and cynicism all through his life, this was a momentous occasion.

But Bhisma objected to the declaration of Karna as a king by Duryodhana who was himself only a prince with no rights. Immediately Duryodhana went to his father and made Dhritarashtra announce Karna as king of Anga. But by this time the sun was already setting, and there could be no further events held. The end of day ensured that Arjuna and Karna did not fight for supremacy. They did not know that their duel was no ordinary fight—it had been ordained aeons back, and in time to come, they would fight the most decisive battle of all—the great war of Kurukshetra.

As a direct fallout of Duryodhana's act of generosity towards a low caste Karna, and his offer of making him a king, Karna joined Duryodhana's camp and followed him faithfully throughout his life. This sense of gratitude would eventually lead Karna to many wrong actions, while the Kauravas earned a great warrior's loyalty to their side as a consequence of Duryodhana's strategic magnanimity.

In the end, even when he learnt of Kunti being his biological mother and got to know that he was the elder brother of the Pandavas, he still did not move away from his chosen path—that of following Duryodhana.

Kunti who was a spectator, realized that Karna was her firstborn when she saw his armour and earrings that shone like gold. She winced at the ridicule heaped on Karna as a charioteer's son but chose to remain quiet and maintain the honour of the royal family. This action of Kunti was perhaps her second biggest sin. For had Kunti spoken up then and there, Karna would have been accepted as one of the Pandavas and in all probability Karna, as the eldest of all, would have been the crown prince—acceptable even to Dhritarashtra since Duryodhana had declared him a friend. This may have averted the war and changed the pages of history.

But Kunti kept mum and the ramifications of her action were suffered by one and all.

chapter 3

Hastinapur

The coming of age of the Kaurava and Pandava princes brought a new dilemma to Dhritarashtra. Bhisma and Vidura counseled Dhritarashtra to announce the crowning of Yudhisthira as *yuvaraj* (crown-prince or king in-the-making) since he was the eldest in the family and had all the virtues to become the crown prince. All the citizens were in favour of this because they knew that Yudhisthira was righteous and Duryodhana was exactly the opposite. Dhritarashtra was torn between his love for his son Duryodhana and his duty towards his brother and the kingdom. Dhritarashtra finally proclaimed Yudhisthira yuvaraj amidst great pomp.

Duryodhana seethed inwardly at the turn of events but on the advice of his uncle Shakuni, masked his feelings and congratulated Yudhisthira in the court. Dhritarashtra suggested that a new palace be built for the Pandavas and Yudhisthira, unaware of any deceit, accepted Duryodhana's offer to build the new abode. Duryodhana and Shakuni used the services of Purochana and got a *Lakshagriha* made—a palace built of flammable materials like wax and lac. Duryodhana and Shakuni had instructed Purochana and his accomplices to set fire to the palace on a new moon night. Vidura learned of Duryodhana's scheme and sent a secret message to Yudhisthira with a miner who dug a tunnel for them to escape. Bhima started a fire before escaping and in the ensuing conflagration, Purochana, his wife and his four accomplices were burnt to death. Seeing the six bodies, everyone assumed that the Pandavas and Kunti were dead. Outwardly, Duryodhana and his brothers mourned the death of the Pandavas but inwardly they were gleeful. Bhisma and Vidura however remained unruffled since they knew that the Pandavas had escaped.

In the meantime they learnt that Drupada had arranged for the swayamvara of his daughter, Draupadi and they left for his kingdom along with other Brahmins who were going there to attend the marriage and receive gifts.

The news of the Pandavas' death had reached far and wide. Drupada was shocked when he heard the news. King Drupada was determined to avenge his humiliation at the hands of Drona. He had realized that for this he needed Arjuna as his ally. So Drupada had planned to get his daughter Draupadi married to Arjuna. He had therefore called for a swayamvara and announced a contest wherein the winner would get the hand of Draupadi. And he was convinced that only Arjuna would be the winner as it was a test of archery. The so-called death of the Pandavas upset Drupada's plans but it was too late to call off the swayamvara.

Several princes from different kingdoms assembled in the court of Drupada on the appointed day. Karna, Duryodhana, Dusshasana and others were there from Hastinapur, and so were Krishna and Balarama from Dwaraka. Duryodhana was no archer, so he requested Karna to win Draupadi for him. When Karna advanced to take up the bow, Draupadi forbade him from participating, citing his low-born status. Karna was once again rebuffed because he was known to be a charioteer's son. The humiliation Karna felt became manifold as the insult came directly from the princess and in front of an assembly of kings. Karna once more realized his birth would follow him like a curse even though he was made a king by Duryodhana.

The Pandavas who were in the guise of Brahmins, too attended the court. Krishna, the cousin of both Pandavas and Kauravas, suggested that the tournament be opened to anyone in the assembly and not only to princes. Taking the cue Drupada made a suitable announcement that the swayamvara was open for all and Arjuna stepped forward. Arjuna successfully hit the target and won Draupadi's hand in marriage. Draupadi garlanded Arjuna and was whisked away by the Pandavas to the forest nearby where Kunti was waiting for them.

Drupada sent his son Drishtadyumna to follow the disguised Pandavas to determine who they were. Drishtadyumna followed them secretly and learning their identity, returned to the palace. Drupada was overjoyed with the news that not only were the Pandavas alive but that

Draupadi had been won by Arjuna. His wish had come true!

Arjuna and Draupadi approached Kunti, for her blessings. Arjuna addressed his mother saying, 'Mother, look what I have brought today. I have participated in a competition and won the prize therein.' Without as much as looking up, Kunti replied as was her wont, 'Dear son, whatever you have won you must share equally with your brothers.'

Horrified, Arjuna shrieked out, 'O Mother! What have you asked me to do? This is an impossible situation. We have vowed to obey you always and now you have asked us to divide a human being amongst ourselves!'

Kunti was aghast when she realized the enormity of her command. But she could not retract her words.

In the meantime Krishna, who had also come to the court of Drupada, explained everything to him. Drupada asked Krishna to bring the Pandavas to his palace so that the marriage could be solemnized with due rites. Krishna hastened to the Pandavas to find them drowned in grief. Krishna, who knew the causal connections, reassured them and brought them all to Drupada's palace. There Krishna told all assembled the story of Draupadi's previous birth as Nalayani and how she had asked for a husband five times. Krishna quoted the marriage of Jatila in ancient times who had simultaneously married ten sages under peculiar circumstances, and suggested that Draupadi marry all five of the brothers. Having convinced all about the propriety of a marriage to more than one man, Krishna oversaw the marriage of Draupadi with the five Pandavas. Later, on the advice of Vedavyasa, the Pandavas came to an understanding that Draupadi would be the wife of one of them for a year while the others would stay separately. During the course of the year with a particular Pandava, none of the other four brothers would enter her chamber. It was a solemn vow with a punishment attached to it in case someone were to break the rule.

When Dhritarashtra learned of all that had happened in Panchala from Duryodhana and Karna, he sent his emissaries and invited the Pandavas to return home. The Pandavas returned to Hastinapur with Kunti and their newlywed wife Draupadi.

Bhisma and Vidura realized that the situation was not favourable for the Pandavas to stay in Hastinapur. So they convinced Dhritarashtra to split the kingdom. A small territory called Khandavaprastha was carved out and given to the Pandavas. Yudhisthira was asked to build a new capital there. Khandavaprastha was the ancient capital from where the entire kingdom had been ruled by great Kuru kings Pururava and Yayati. Neither the Pandavas nor the Kauravas were happy with the arrangement. The Pandavas did not want to leave Hastinapur and the Kauravas did not like the idea of giving anything, even wasteland, to the Pandavas.

On arrival at the old capital, the Pandavas saw that it was densely forested and not suitable for habitation. Once when Arjuna and Krishna were wandering in the forest discussing how to build the new capital, Agni, the god of fire, assumed the form of an old Brahmin, approached Arjuna and asked for help. When Arjuna readily agreed, Agni revealed himself and said to the surprised Arjuna, 'I wanted your vow of help, hence the disguise of an old Brahmin. I am suffering from indigestion because of the innumerable *yagnas* that have been performed. I need to consume this forest along with its inhabitants so that the fire in my belly is cured. Several medicinal plants grow in this forest.'

Agni had strategically sought Arjuna's help since Indra, Arjuna's father, was the friend of the snake Takshaka who dwelt in the forest along with his family. Indra would prevent Agni from swallowing the forest by dousing him with rain and thunder showers. With Arjuna on guard fighting Indra and preventing him from causing showers, and Krishna stopping the inhabitants from fleeing, Agni devoured the forest. Takshaka was away from home and escaped death. His wife and son were, however, consumed by Agni. When Takshaka got to know of everything, he vowed that he would kill Arjuna at a suitable time. After the burning down of the forest, the Pandavas were able to rebuild the old city with the help of Maya. As a mark of gratitude, Agni presented a chariot with horses yoked to it, a magnificent bow named Gandiva with two quivers of inexhaustible arrows to Arjuna, a conch called Pancajanya to Krishna, and a huge mace to Bhima. None of these gifts were ordinary, coming as they were from Agni, the god of fire.

Soon after settling down in the new capital, one day, in order to help a Brahmin get back his stolen cows, Arjuna entered Draupadi's room to take his bow while she was with another husband. As a consequence, Arjuna had to leave the palace and go on a pilgrimage for a year, having broken his vow and violating the condition stipulated by Vedavyasa during their marriage.

During these wanderings, he landed in Dwaraka and helped by Krishna, eloped and married Subhadra, his sister. Krishna, though a cousin of both the Kauravas and Pandavas, became more closely tied with the Pandavas first by being the nephew of Kunti and now by Subhadra's marriage to Arjuna. The Pandavas held him in high esteem and sought his advice and support at all times. He became their mentor and guided them throughout their lives on the path of righteousness.

The Pandavas had a new palace built at Khandavaprastha by a demon named Maya who was Vishwakarma's equal in architecture. When Agni was about to consume the forest of Khandavavana, Maya, who was living there, took refuge in Arjuna and Krishna and hence was saved from the fire. As a token of his gratitude, Maya built the palace with many ingenious devices like moving walls and mirror images, creating such illusions that anyone new to it would be confused of what was real and what was not. The palace had no equal on earth—it was the palace of illusions!

Yudhisthira sought the advice of Krishna to perform the *Rajasuya yagna* which meant establishment of his supremacy over all kings, defeating them in battle, if necessary. Krishna told Yudhisthira about Jarasandha, the monarch of Magadha, whose capital was Girivraja. Jarasandha was a mighty king and a worshipper of Bhairava, the terrible aspect of Siva. He had conquered many kings and held them in prison, planning a great yagna to sacrifice them to his deity. He needed hundred kings for the sacrifice and had been able to imprison only eighty-four. Krishna advised Yudhisthira to conquer Jarasandha, free the imprisoned kings, thereby gaining their loyalty, and then perform the Rajasuya yagna.

Accordingly Bhima, Arjuna and Krishna went to the kingdom of Jarasandha in disguise. Jarasandha, unaware of their identity, welcomed them into the palace. They took a promise from Jarasandha that he would give what they asked for. After that, at night, they declared their true selves and challenged Jarasandha to a duel, allowing him to choose his opponent. Jarasandha chose to fight with Bhima and they engaged in a hand to hand combat. Bhima and Jarasandha were equally matched and fought continuously for thirteen days while Krishna and Arjuna looked on with hope and anxiety. On the fourteenth day Jarasandha's energy began to fail. Bhima caught his legs and tore him asunder. But even before Bhima could roar out his victory the two halves came together and joined to bring back Jarasandha in full form with renewed vigour. Bhima repeated his act of vanquishing Jarasandha but each time the two halves would join together. Bhima was unaware of the secret of Jarasandha's birth.

༄

Jarasandha was the son of King Brihadratha who had remained childless for a long time. Brihadratha approached

Sage Kaushika who gave him a mango with magical powers and his blessings. He asked the king to give the fruit to his wife, and a son would be born. Since King Brihadratha had two wives and he loved both equally, he cut the mango into two halves and gave his two wives a piece each. When the queens gave birth, it was not a normal baby that was born to each, but strangely, each of them bore half of a son—as if equal and complementary halves of one baby were shared by both. This was so because each queen had only eaten half the fruit that the sage had given as boon.

The horrified queens instructed their servants to wrap up the two halves and throw them away immediately, afraid of some terrible omen or curse.

A demoness called Jaraa chanced on the bundle and on opening it, found the two halves. With her power, Jaraa merged the halves together the right way to form a beautiful child. The demoness did not want to kill the infant. She took the guise of a woman, and taking the baby to the king, told him what had happened. The king was delighted and immediately accepted the baby as his son. The child was named Jarasandha since he was joined together by Jaraa. He grew up to be an enormously strong and ferocious warrior—demonic traits had got into him through Jaraa's power. However, Jarasandha's body had only one weakness—the line at the center where the two halves had joined was vulnerable. It could be split into two if sufficient force was applied.

Bhima continued to fight Jarasandha to no avail. Finally Bhima wearied of this task and looked at Krishna for help. Krishna indicated that the two halves should be thrown in opposite directions, by splitting a straw into two and throwing the pieces in opposite directions. Bhima understood Krishna's hint and did the same with Jarasandha's body. The two pieces were no longer aligned and though they came together, they could not form a whole. Thus Jarasandha met his end. The numerous kings who were held in captivity by Jarasandha were freed and they all accepted Yudhisthira's supremacy.

At the end of the Rajasuya yagna Yudhisthira approached Bhisma with these words: 'Grandsire, I seek your advice. As is the custom I need to honor all the guests but first of all, I need to choose the one most worthy, and honour him at the beginning (*agrapooja*). Please tell me who is the most worthy of all'.

Bhisma replied immediately, 'There is no one other than Krishna who should adorn this postion. Honour him with agrapooja and you would have honoured all'. This infuriated some of those present in the hall including the Kauravas who chose to keep quiet. King Sisupala and his brother Dantavakra openly opposed the choice. They spoke harshly and began to leave the hall. Yudhisthira tried his best to mollify them but they began to hurl abuses at Krishna. Finally, after hearing out one hundred verbal abuses from Sisupala as he had vowed to tolerate, Krishna cut the brothers' heads off with his discus. Krishna was then duly honoured and the yagna completed.

After the yagna, Duryodhana wanted to see the new palace

in its entirety. Though Yudhisthira offered to accompany him so as to explain the artifices and illusions that adorned the palace, Duryodhana refused his offer and went alone. At one place, Duryodhana mistook a glassy surface for water and stepped on it carefully. Realizing his mistake, he determined to walk on such surfaces without care. Immediately, he stepped into a pool that looked like a solid surface and was completely drenched. Unfortunately for him, Draupadi and her attendants happened to witness this. Seeing Duryodhana befooled by the illusion and slipping into the pool, her attendants could not control their laughter. Draupadi chided them but this only added salt to Duryodhana's injury and he assumed that it was Draupadi who had laughed and was then ridiculing him by chiding the attendants. Then and there Duryodhana vowed that he would humiliate the Pandavas, especially Draupadi, who had dared to laugh at him.

Duryodhana related all that had happened to Shakuni and Dusshasana, and conspired with them. Shakuni offered a masterplan to take away all the possessions of the Pandavas and debase them. He suggested inviting Yudhisthira for a game of dice wherein Shakuni would play on behalf of Duryodhana. Shakuni possessed a pair of dice made from his father's thigh bones which would roll in any manner Shakuni desired, thereby giving him the numbers he wanted. Shakuni was therefore invincible when he played with his dice. Yudhisthira would be prodded to wager his kingdom, his wealth, themselves and even Draupadi, and Shakuni would win them all. Thus Duryodhana would come into possession of all that the Pandavas had without waging war, and he would be able to exact revenge for the insult suffered at Draupadi's hands.

Duryodhana got his father Dhritarashtra to send an invitation through Vidura, knowing that Yudhisthira could not refuse, as it was unbecoming of a king or Kshatriya to refuse an invitation from a king to play dice. Vidura played the messenger but warned Yudhisthira against accepting the invite. But Yudhisthira was duty bound, following *rajadharma*, and so the Pandavas, along with Draupadi and Kunti, came to Hastinapur.

Initially, Shakuni allowed Yudhisthira to win a couple of games which made him believe he had a winning streak. Then the stakes were slowly raised game after game, and Yudhisthira lost all that was his. Nagged by Shakuni's taunts and egged on by gambler's hope, Yudhisthira pawned his brothers, one by one. Then he pawned himself. But every roll of dice favoured Shakuni. Finally, in the hope of winning back everything with one last roll of dice, Yudhisthira wagered Draupadi, wife of the five Pandavas. Never for once did he pause to reflect on his actions and their repercussions—so desperate was he to win back everything he had lost. And then he lost her too. Yudhisthira, who was the embodiment of Dharma and righteousness, had slipped from the chosen path, and this act unspooled all the evil that was to follow.

Duryodhana seized the moment and declaring that all the Pandavas and Draupadi had become his slaves, sought to insult them by asking them to disrobe themselves and prostrate before him. He ordered Dusshasana that Draupadi be brought to the court; when she refused, she was forcibly dragged by her hair from the ladies quarters by Dusshasana.

No one in the assembly opened his mouth and resisted. None supported her case including her own husbands who had become slaves to Duryodhana. Duryodhana unbared his thigh to indicate that she sit on his lap as she now belonged to him. Draupadi's pleas went unheard till it turned to rage as she railed that there was none who supported the cause of virtuousness (*na saa sabhaa yatra na santi vrddhaah, vrddhaa na te ye na vadanti dharmam*). Finally when Dusshasana tried to disrobe her forcibly, Draupadi sought refuge in Krishna, who, by his infinite power, kept Draupadi clothed even as Dusshasana kept pulling off her sarees.

Bhima could not control his anger and rising from his seat proclaimed, 'I, Bhima, hereby vow to kill Dusshasana, tear his heart out and drink his blood. Duryodhana has taunted Draupadi by slapping his thighs. I, therefore, will break his thighs with this very mace of mine.'

Bhima's terrible vow echoed in the hall and pierced the ears of Dhritarashtra who was cursing his sightlessness till then. When Draupadi declared that she would burn them down with her power of penance, Dhritarashtra realized that he had allowed his son to go too far, and fearing Draupadi's curses, rose from his throne and made attempts to mollify her. He asked Bhisma, Drona, Vidura and others to come forward and salvage the situation. They advised him to apologize to Draupadi and give her boons. Draupadi asked for the freedom of her husbands and the return of their kingdom. Dhritarashtra granted her wishes and the Pandavas, Draupadi and Kunti left for Indraprastha to the chagrin of Duryodhana and his coterie.

In the meantime, after completion of the Rajasuya yagna at Indraprastha, Krishna had returned to Dwaraka to find that King Salva had besieged Dwaraka. King Salva was King Sisupala's friend. Hearing of Sisupala's death, King Salva had attacked Dwaraka.

chapter 4

Duryodhana's Treachery

After the Pandavas and others left for Indraprastha, there was a furore in the court of Hastinapur. Bhisma, Drona, and Vidura condemned Dhritarashtra for having allowed Duryodhana to behave in such a heinous manner. They were aghast at Duryodhana's humiliation of his cousins and Dhritarashtra turning a blind eye, figuratively. Duryodhana was adamant and continued to argue that he had only avenged his insult by Draupadi. Duryodhana declared that he was the rightful heir to the Hastinapur throne and Yudhisthira must abdicate his right or be made to lose it in some way to Duryodhana. Towards this end, Duryodhana persuaded Dhritarashtra once again to invite the Pandavas for another game of dice. Despite protests from the Kuru elders—Bhisma and Vidura—Dhritarashtra succumbed to his son's influence and sent an envoy. Dhritarashtra, born blind, was also blind when Duryodhana was concerned.

Even before the Pandavas could reach their palace in

Indraprastha, the envoy conveyed the message sent by Dhritarasthra. Duty bound, they returned to Hastinapur to play yet another game of dice. This time the wager was that the loser would have to spend twelve years in exile and one year in hiding. In case of being discovered while in hiding, a successive twelve years in exile and thirteenth year in hiding was mandated. Duryodhana was convinced that he would be able to find them in their thirteenth year, thus extending their exile repeatedly, and making him king forever. As planned, this time also Shakuni threw the dice for Duryodhana's play. Yudhisthira should have objected and refused to play such a game. Unfortunately, he was again silent and allowed himself to be overtaken by the situation. By the connivance of Shakuni, Duryodhana won the game again and the Pandavas with Draupadi left for the forest leaving their mother Kunti in the care of Vidura.

chapter 5

The Exile

The Pandavas and Draupadi spent twelve years in the forest. They had many adventures and escapades and formed alliances in preparation for an impending conflict with the Kauravas. On Sage Vedavyasa's advice, Arjuna went to the Himalayas to practice austerities and obtain weapons from the gods as boons. He prayed fervently to Siva and obtained the mighty *Pashupata astra*. After obtaining the Pashupata astra, Arjuna went to his father Indra for help. As soon as he entered the heavens, he was accosted by Urvashi who wanted him to spend a night with her. Arjuna prostrated before her and said, 'Forgive me. You belong to Indra who is my father and thereby you become equivalent to my mother. I can only revere you in the form of my mother.' But Urvashi was enraged. 'How dare you scorn me? You do not understand a woman's feelings. Since you reject a woman's passion, I curse you to suffer a woman's body!'

Arjuna begged forgiveness but Urvashi was firm. Finally

Indra stepped in and asked Urvashi to modify her curse to last one year only. When Urvashi left, Indra told Arjuna that Urvashi's curse would prove useful when he needed to remain incognito during the thirteenth year of exile.

Years passed in this manner. One day Bhima went hunting alone. He chanced upon a python and was marvelling at its size. Before he could realize the imminent danger, the python had wrapped itself around him. The coils of the python were so strong that even Bhima who had the strength of a thousand elephants, could not do anything. Then Bhima addressed the python thus: 'I am Bhima the Pandava, brother of Yudhishtira. I have tackled several lions, tigers, elephants easily but this strength of yours defies me. Who are you really, O Snake?'

The python calmly replied, 'I was the great king Nahusha of the Ikshvaku race. Due to my arrogance I was cursed by Sage Agastya and have fallen from being human to becoming a reptile. When I repented and asked for grace, I was told that one day King Yudhishtira will come and be my saviour. Maybe today is that day. I do not want to kill you. But I have to do it because it is part of my curse.'

In the meantime, Yudhishtira had a premonition that evil had befallen Bhima. So he came in search of Bhima and found him in the coils of a huge python. Yudhishtira realized that this was no ordinary python and introducing himself to the snake, begged him to release Bhima. The python revealed his true self as Nahusha and told him about his curse and how he could achieve redemption only if Yudhishtira answered his questions correctly. Yudhisthira agreed.

The python began his questions on ethics and Yudhishtira being the embodiment of Dharma, was able to answer all his questions successfully. Immediately, a divine chariot came down from the skies and Nahusha shed his serpent skin, reassuming his earlier majestic form. Bhima was free. Nahusha blessed Yudhishtira, climbed the chariot and left while the brothers embraced each other in joy before returning to the hermitage.

Though it was known that the Pandavas were suffering in the forest, Duryodhana wanted to see their difficulties and enjoy their distress. Hence he kept thinking of ways to do so. One day on Karna's suggestion, he asked his father Dhritarashtra's permission to go to Dwaitavana for annual stock-taking of cows. Dhritarashtra did not agree as he knew that the Pandavas were dwelling in the nearby forest and he had a suspicion that Duryodhana had some evil plans. Finally, Shakuni and Duryodhana overcame Dhritarashtra's misgivings and the Kauravas reached Dwaitavana with a great army and many followers. They camped about four miles away from the Pandavas' abode, took stock of the cows, spent time in hunting and other sylvan sports. While hunting, Duryodhana and his party reached an attractive pond and decided to indulge in some fun there. However, Chitrasena, the Gandharva king, had already encamped in the neighbourhood of the pool and prevented Duryodhana's men from putting up their camp. This annoyed Duryodhana who ordered his men to destroy the encampment of Chitrasena.

Chitrasena was able to overpower Karna and Shakuni and took Duryodhana and some other Kauravas captive. Some of Duryodhana's men escaped and reaching the Pandava hermitage, took refuge. Hearing what had happened, Yudhishtira asked Bhima to rescue the captive Kauravas from Chitrasena and his people. Bhima and Arjuna refused, but at Yudhishtira's insistence, they rallied the Kaurava troops and led them to fight Chitrasena who, however, had no desire to fight the Pandavas. Chitrasena released the captives at Arjuna's behest and the dishonoured Kauravas returned to Hastinapur. Instead of being able to enjoy the predicament of the Pandavas living in the forest, Duryodhana had disgraced himself further. Instead of being grateful for their help in saving him, Duryodhana's ego made him feel humiliated by the Pandavas' strength.

One day Sage Durvasa came to Hastinapur palace. On Shakuni's advice, Duryodhana served the sage with a show of much humility and devotion and pleased him so that Sage Durvasa blessed Duryadhana with a boon. Immediately Duryodhana's evil mind hatched a plan and instead of asking for a boon, he requested the sage to visit the Pandavas and bless them—but only late in the afternoon. Duryodhana thought that the Pandavas would not be able to serve the sage as they were living in inhospitable conditions and would thus incur the wrath of the sage. Sage Durvasa saw nothing amiss and reached the Pandavas with his retinue of devotees. The Pandavas were resting after their midday meal. They welcomed the sage and honoured him and his disciples. The sage said that they would perform their ablutions and then wanted to be served food. Hearing this Draupadi and the Pandavas became terrified of the sage's wrath as they knew they had no food left to serve.

Yudhisthira remembered the *Akshaya paatra* he had received as a boon from Surya when they had just set out on the exile. On the advice of their guru Dhaumya, Yudhishtira had worshipped the Sun-god with intense concentration and devotion until Surya appeared before him. Surya did not ask Yudhishtira what he wanted. Instead he blessed him, gave him a copper vessel with a boon. 'I am pleased with your devotion. I know you will be living in the forest during your exile and food will be hard to come by. This pot is called the Akshaya paatra and will be of use. Draupadi will get all the food she needs when she begins to serve from this vessel. But take care to see that Draupadi eats last, for after she completes her meal this vessel will become empty until it is time for the next meal.'

Yudhisthira went to Draupadi to see if she had finished her meal. He was horrified to see that the vessel had been cleaned and kept aside. When Draupadi realized the situation they were in, she immediately prayed earnestly to Krishna asking him to come to their help and deliver them from the situation. At once Krishna appeared before her but instead of enquiring about her, said, 'I am hungry, please give me some food.' Draupadi broke down and started weeping. 'Please do not say such words. There is no food in the house. The power of the Akshaya paatra is exhausted. Sage Durvasa and his disciples will be here any moment. And you try me thus.' Without seeming to hear her anguished pleas, Krishna repeated, 'I am terribly hungry. Do not give me any excuses. Please fetch the Akshaya paatra here immediately. I will check it for myself.' Draupadi brought the copper pot. Lo and behold, there was a tiny grain of rice sticking to the rim of the vessel. Krishna extracted it and put it into his mouth. He then exclaimed, 'I am full and satiated.'

Draupadi felt ashamed that she had not cleaned the pot well, not realizing that this had saved the situation. Krishna then asked Bhima to escort Sage Durvasa and his devotees from the river to partake of the meal. Bhima was astounded but without a word he hastened to the river where the sage and his followers were bathing. He found them all resting under the trees with pleased satiety. Bhima was surprised. The disciples told their guru Sage Durvasa, 'We feel well-fed and cannot eat anything more. Please forgive us.' He told Bhima, 'Please tell Yudhishtira to forgive us. We cannot eat anything at your place.' Durvasa, with his divine insight, had realized what had happened and went away satisfied. When Bhima returned and related all this, everyone realized how Krishna had saved them. Since the entire universe is contained in Krishna, his satisfaction with one grain of rice satisfied the hunger of all, including Sage Durvasa and his disciples.

It was the final year of exile of the Pandavas. One day the brothers went hunting, leaving Draupadi with their preceptor Sage Dhaumya. While they were away, King Jayadratha of Sindhu and his friend who were passing by, saw Draupadi standing alone near the doorway of the hermitage. Smitten by her beauty Jayadratha abducted her and rode away. Dhaumya could not do anything against them and he sat waiting for the Pandavas to return. When the Pandavas returned and learned about Draupadi's abduction, they set off to bring her back. They fought with Jayadratha's army and routed it. When Jayadratha ran away, they went to his chariot and freed Draupadi. Bhima and Arjuna caught Jayadratha and having defeated him in a duel, cut his hair short so that everyone who looked at him would know his humiliation. They did not kill Jayadratha as Yudhishtira had forbidden them from doing so since Jayadratha was married to Dusshala, and was therefore, the son-in-law of Hastinapur.

Jayadratha went away, insulted and humiliated in a terrible frame of mind. Like Duryodhana, he did not realize it was his own act of abduction that was heinous, but he raged at the Pandavas for having brought this humiliation on himself. Jayadratha did not return to his kingdom but sat in penance and prayed till Siva appeared before him. When asked what was it that he was praying for so earnestly, Jayadratha replied, 'O Lord Siva, give me the boon that I will defeat the Pandavas in war.' Siva said that such a boon could not be granted since the Pandavas were sons of gods, invincible and protected by Vishnu himself. But Jayadratha would not let his austerities go to naught and kept asking for his boon. Finally Siva gave the boon, saying, 'By my boon you will be invincible for one day but you will still not be able to defy Arjuna and Krishna.' Jayadratha was not happy with the boon but consoled himself that he could at least defy Bhima and the other brothers even though it would be only for one day. He went home and bode his time for revenge.

During the final months of their exile, a Brahmin came to them for help. A deer had come into his hut and carried away the *arani*—sticks used to make the sacrificial fire—that had got entangled in its antlers. He needed the arani back and the deer had to be hunted. The Pandavas set out in pursuit but they could not locate the deer. Fatigued by hunger and thirst they rested under a tree. Since Yudhishtira was thirsty, Nakula set out to get water. He found a lake nearby but when he was about to drink the water a voice said, 'Do not drink this water or carry it unless you answer my questions.' Not seeing anyone around, Nakula ignored the voice. He had just touched the water when he fell dead. Having waited for Nakula for a long time, Yudhishtira sent Sahadeva in search of Nakula. He too faced the same fate. Arjuna and Bhima were sent in search by turn but nobody returned. Finally Yudhishtira himself walked towards the lake to find all his brothers lying dead on the edge of the lake. He was horrified and did not know what to do. After grieving for some time he decided to quench his thirst and approached the lake. He heard the voice that all his brothers had disregarded. Yudhishtira paused and looked around. 'I warned your brothers but they did not listen to me. You too will die if you try to drink water without answering my questions and obtaining my permission. I am the yaksha who owns this lake,' the voice said. Yudhishtira immediately replied, 'O Great One! Please reveal yourself. You are indeed great as you have killed all my brothers whom I had thought to be invincible.'

The yaksha appeared and Yudhishtira said, 'I am thankful to you for having shown yourself. I will not disregard your words and drink the water since this lake belongs to you. Please ask me the questions and I will try my best to find answers for them.'

The yaksha began asking questions about ethics and Yudhishtira began answering them. When he had answered them all, the yaksha said, 'I am pleased with your humility and knowledge. I now grant you a boon. I can bring back only one of your brothers to life, which one will it be? Choose wisely.'

Yudhishtira thought awhile and said, 'Please restore the life of Nakula.' When the yaksha expressed his amazement at Yudhishtra's choice, he explained it thus: 'My father had two wives—Kunti and Madri. I want both their children to be alive since I love them both equally. I am the son of Kunti and Nakula is the son of Madri. This is the reason for my choice.' The yaksha was pleased with the righteousness of Yudhishtira and gave the boon of life to all the Pandavas. Yudhishtira embraced them all and then falling at the feet of the yaksha asked him to reveal his true self. The yaksha gave up his form and the illustrious Dharmaraja stood before them. He said 'I am pleased with you, my son. Your name will be remembered in aftertimes. I stole the sticks because I wanted to draw you near this lake and test you. You can take back the sticks to give to the Brahmin. I also grant you another boon. Your exile of twelve years is over. The last and most difficult year is on you. I bless all of you that no one will be able to recognize your true identities when you are disguised.'

In the thirteenth year they spent their time disguised, in the kingdom of Virata. Yudhisthira was disguised as courtier Kanka, Bhima as cook Valala, Arjuna used Urvashi's curse by which he would have the form of a woman for a year, and disguised himself as Brihannala, a dance teacher to Virata's daughter Uttaraa. Nakula chose to be a horse trainer Damagranthi, and Sahadeva a cowherd Tantripala. Draupadi was disguised as a *Sairandhri*—the queen's handmaid.

In Virata's court, his brother-in-law Keechaka held sway as the commander-in-chief of all the armies. He was a valiant warrior but his lust for women was a cause of concern to all, though none opposed him out of fear. Keechaka chanced upon Draupadi, in servant guise, and lusted for her. Despite her pleas that she was a married woman and her husbands were Gandharvas, Keechaka insisted that she serve him by threatening to possess her forcibly if she denied him. Draupadi approached King Virata for protection but King Virata did not have the courage to oppose his brother-in-law and expressed his helplessness. Keechaka then forced his sister to help him by sending Draupadi to his service with wine. There Keechaka again expressed his feelings for Draupadi but she continued to refuse him. Finally Draupadi agreed to meet him in the dead of the night. Draupadi enlisted Bhima's help. Bhima dressed as a woman took Draupadi's place and met Keechaka. There Bhima revealed himself and drew Keechaka into a combat. He crushed Keechaka into a ball of flesh. The lustful, drunk with power Keechaka met the end he deserved.

The news of Keechaka's death reached Hastinapur. Shakuni immediately guessed that it had to be Bhima, in disguise, who had killed Keechaka. In order to flush out the Pandavas, Duryodhana sent his army in support of King Susharma. The plan was that Susharma, king of Trigartas, would attack Virata's kingdom and take away the cattle-wealth. All other Kuru chiefs would join from other directions. Since King Virata would not be able to face the combined armies of the kings, the Pandavas who were in his refuge would be forced to help him out. They would have to come out of their disguises and fight on Virata's side. Since their identity would become known before the completion of the *Ajnaatavaasa* (one year in hiding) Duryodhana would be able to send them away to the forest for another period of twelve years exile followed by a year in hiding.

As expected, to save Virata's honour, Brihannala, or Arjuna, offered to be the charioteer for Uttara, the crown prince leading Virata's army. Uttara was a very young boy and not courageous. As soon as the chariot came face to face with the huge armies arrayed to fight, he jumped off the chariot and began to run homewards. Arjuna turned the chariot and catching up with him, revealed his true self to prince Uttara. Arjuna then went to a tree near a burial ground. There Uttara retrieved Arjuna's Gandiva bow which he had hidden along with the weapons of his brothers inside a hollow tree, and they set off to face the Kaurava armies. He fought Duryodhana's armies single-handedly and routed them. Arjuna used the '*Sanmmohana*' incantation and put everyone to sleep—Bhisma, Drona, Kripa, Aswathama, Karna and other warriors. In the meanwhile Duryodhana had fled the battlefield. Prince Uttara snatched the feathers in the crowns of all the warriors except Bhisma, Kripa and Drona and brought them back to the city as a sign of having won the battle. Duryodhana's plan was foiled when he was made to realize that his calculations were wrong and that Arjuna had revealed himself only because the last day of the thirteenth year had ended the previous night. After returning victorious from the battle, the Pandavas revealed themselves to King Virata who embraced them and was very happy to have been able to provide them shelter in their time of need.

He also offered his daughter Uttaraa in marriage to Arjuna who politely refused saying that Uttaraa was like a daughter to him as he was her dance teacher. In turn he requested her hand for his son Abhimanyu. The marriage of Abhimanyu and Uttaraa was performed duly with great pomp and splendour.

When the Pandavas declared the completion of the thirteenth year, they sent Krishna as their ambassador for peace and asked for just five villages instead of a kingdom. But

Duryodhana, incapable as he was of any righteous action, refused infamously thus: 'I will not give to Pandavas even so much land as is covered by the tip of a needle.' Duryodhana even ordered his soldiers to capture Krishna and shackle him. However, Krishna revealed his true self and none could even go near him. His shining appearance blinded all except Bhisma, Drona and Vidura who prostrated themselves, having realized that Krishna was displaying his supreme form, or *Virat Rupa*.

Dhritarashtra prayed to Krishna and received the boon of sight to see the divine form of Krishna. Once Krishna assumed his human form, he offered Dhritarashtra the choice to retain his sight. But Dhritarashtra refused saying, 'O Krishna, I have realized that you are the Supreme Power. After having seen you, I do not wish to see anything else that belongs to this world. Please take away the power of sight that you have given me and let me remain in darkness as I have lived all these years.'

Krishna returned to the Pandavas with the answer that war was inevitable. Yudhisthira was however sad as war meant killing of their cousins, friends, and relatives. Among the Pandavas, while Yudhisthira was vehemently against the war, Draupadi who had spent each moment of each day of the thirteen years in exile with the only thought of annihilation of Duryodhana and his brothers, was infuriated with Yudhisthira's meek approach. Bhima was totally in agreement with Draupadi and was thirsting for revenge. Arjuna was ambivalent, while the twins did not express their opinions in deference to Yudhisthira. Draupadi pleaded with Krishna for justice and he gave her his word. However, he made all efforts for a peaceful resolution.

To Yudhisthira, Krishna quoted a *shastravakya* (saying of shastra) that Duryodhana and his wicked followers need to be killed since they had committed heinous crimes all these years, such as trying to kill the Pandavas by putting fire to their living quarters, poisoning Bhima, snatching away their wealth and kingdom by deceit. The Kauravas had even tried to usurp the wife of the Pandavas in the deceitful game of dice—*agnido garadas caiva shastrapaanih dhanaapahah/ ksetradaaraharashcaiva shadaite hyaatataayinah.*

℘

Once war was declared the two sides began to prepare themselves by amassing armies and allies. Kurukshetra was chosen as the battlefield. The kingdoms of Panchala headed by Drupada, Kasi, Kekaya, Magadha, Matsya, Chedi, Pandyas, Kalinga, and the Yadus of Mathura and some other clans like the Parama Kambojas were allied with the Pandavas. The allies of the Kauravas included the kings of Pragjyotisha, Anga, Sindhudesa, Mahishmati, Avanti in Madhyadesa, Madra, Gandhara, Kambojas and many others. Before war was declared, Balarama had expressed his unhappiness at the developing conflict and left for a pilgrimage; thus he did not take part in the battle itself. Rukmi, brother of Rukmini, too did not take part in the battle since no one invited him to join their side. Both Arjuna and Duryodhana approached

Krishna for help as Krishna was a cousin to both. Krishna offered them a choice—his mighty army or himself. Arjuna chose Krishna as his charioteer while a jubilant Duryodhana, believing that strength lay in the army, was happy to accept Krishna's army. Duryodhana hardly knew that victory lay on the side of Pandavas who were always righteous (*yato dharmah tato jayah*). Krishna is the embodiment of Dharma and victory follows the side that Krishna takes:*yatra yogiishvarah krsnah...tatra shriir vijayo bhuutih*).

//
Part V
The Great War

chapter 1

Bhisma's Leadership

The battle at Kurukshetra began and both armies arrayed themselves against each other. Rules of combat had been discussed and agreed upon by both sides, important among them being that any fight should be between equals, the battle would conclude at sunset every day, and an unarmed warrior would not be attacked or killed. Yudhishtira appointed Drupada, Shikandi, Dhristadyumna, Virata, Satyaki, Chekitana and Bhima as generals. Dhristadyumna was also anointed supreme commander of the Pandava forces. Bhisma was made commander-in-chief of the Kaurava army. Drona, Kripa, Aswathama, Bhoorisravas and Salya were with him. Bhisma forbade Karna from fighting under his leadership as he was a charioteer's son.

The previous night of the Kurukshetra war, Sage Vedavyasa met Dhritarshtra and made him aware of the result of the war—in which the Kauravas and all fighting on their side would die. The sage offered Dhritarashtra the boon of sight to watch the battle but the king refused it. Instead, he asked for someone to relate the happenings of the battle. Sage Vedavyasa appointed Sanjaya, and granted him the boon of divine sight—Sanjaya would see and hear everything as if he were physically present everywhere on the battlefield. By Vedavyasa's boon Sanjaya would know no fatigue and would be able to relate everything in minute details to Dhritarashtra.

Yudhisthira, before giving the clarion call for the start of the war, walked across the battlefield accompanied by his brothers and Krishna. The Pandavas took the blessings first of their grandsire Bhisma, then from Guru Drona and finally from Kulaguru Kripa. Yudhishtira expressed his sorrow for having to fight them. He also made the final appeal for anyone who might wish to come to his side and Yuyutsu came over. Then conches were blown and the battle was set to begin.

Before the battle began Arjuna asked Krishna to take him to the centre of the battlefield so that he could see the enemy ranks. When Krishna reached there, Arjuna saw his relatives and loved ones and was stricken with grief that he had to take arms against them. He refused to fight and threw down his bow, much to the Kauravas' delight and the Pandavas' dismay, and pleaded with Krishna to stop the war. It is then that Krishna explained to Arjuna that he was wrong in grieving in this manner. Arjuna did not know that he was only killing the body and not the soul (*aatmaa*) which is eternal. Death is like any other state in life such as childhood, youth, and old age. It is like changing into new clothes, throwing away the old ones (*vaasaamsi jiirnaani yathaa vihaaya navaani grhnaati naro aparaani*). The soul has neither birth nor death (*na jaayate mriyate vaa kadaacit*), it is untouched by any of the five elements that compose this material world. Krishna made him realize his duty with his exposition of the Bhagavad Gita or 'Word of God'. The inspired Arjuna decided to perform his duty to the Supreme God and took up the Gandiva, his signature bow. He said, 'I am ready to act as you enjoin me to do' (karisye vacanam tava), and requested Krishna to return him to the ranks.

On the first day the Pandava army was arranged in a formation called Vajra. This was the favourite arrangement of Indra and it got its name from him. Many were killed and huge losses to horses, elephants and foot soldiers were suffered by both sides. Both sons of King Virata, Uttara and Sveta died on the first day. Uttara was killed by King Salya and Sveta by grandsire. Duryodhana was delirious with joy. Bhisma fought so ferociously that Duryodhana was convinced that the battle would be over in no time and he would get Karna to kill the Pandavas. The second day brought losses to the Kaurava army due to Arjuna's fierce fighting though both the armies had chosen the Krauncha vyuha (heron formation). Bhisma laid his army in an eagle formation on the third day. To counter this, Dhristadyumna arrayed the Pandava army in the shape of a crescent. Though Bhisma was fighting his best, Duryodhana kept reproaching him with harsh words, accusing him of partiality towards the Pandavas. Spurred by Duryodhana's words Bhisma destroyed all who came in his way like a forest fire. Arjuna and Bhisma engaged in a long drawn out fight but Arjuna's mind was not in it. One of Bhisma's arrows almost grazed Krishna. Seeing this, Krishna got off the chariot and went towards Bhisma shouting, 'I will kill you myself with my discus if Arjuna does not want to fight against you.' Bhisma was overjoyed and falling to his knees said, 'I bow to you, O Lord of the three worlds! Death at your hands will mean complete salvation. May your hands take my life.' Arjuna seeing that Krishna was about to break his word of not using weapons in the war came running towards him and stopped Krishna by promising not to flinch any more. Arjuna thus persuaded Krishna to return to the chariot. Arjuna then attacked the Kaurava army furiously and thousands were slain by him on that day. On the fourth day Bhima killed eight of Duryodhana's brothers. Seeing this havoc caused by Bhima, Bhisma sent Bhagadatta to fight with Bhima. Bhagadatta, the king of Pragjyotisha, hurled a terrible javelin at Bhima. The impact of the javelin made Bhima faint. Seeing this, Ghatotkacha came to Bhima's rescue. Bhisma then made his armies retire early though dusk was yet to set, as he knew that Ghatotkacha's powers would increase with the setting sun.

The fifth day saw the Kaurava army arranged in the Makara Vyuha (crocodile formation) while the Pandavas chose to array their army in a hawk formation. Both armies had heavy losses. On the sixth day the Pandavas arrayed themselves in Matsya vyuha (fish formation) while the Kauravas made a Krauncha vyuha (heron formation). Bhisma arranged the Kaurava armies in Mandala vyuha (circular formation) on the seventh day, while the Pandavas chose to use the Vajra vyuha. Sankha, the third son of Virata fell this day while fighting against Drona. At the end of the seventh day both sides were not jubilant as both armies had suffered heavy losses. Bhisma spread the army like the waves of the sea on the eighth day, while Yudhishtira asked Dhristadyumna to arrange their army in the Sringataka (horns) formation. On the eighth day Bhima killed eight of Duryodhana's brothers in the early part of the day. By that Duryodhana had lost twenty-four of his brothers to Bhima. Nine days passed and both sides suffered heavy losses. Bhisma took on an invincible *avatara* and fell upon the Pandavas armies. The Pandavas were terrified for the first time in their lives. Yudhisthira sought Krishna's advice. He said, 'Our grandfather Bhisma is unstoppable. I believe that he has a boon wherein he can choose his time of death. But how do we impose upon him to do so. Else killing him is impossible. Please help us.' Krishna smilingly answered, 'Only Bhisma will be able to answer your question. You must ask him and he will help you.'

That night Yudhisthira met Bhisma and asked him to help them win the war. Bhisma replied, 'I know what you want. Unless I die, you cannot win. I will tell you a secret. I will not fight a woman. I will give up my arms if faced with a woman.' Yudhisthira returned puzzled.

Women were not allowed to fight so he could not think how he could bring a lady to attack Bhisma. When he discussed this with the others, Dhristadyumna, said, 'Why don't we send Shikhandi to fight Bhisma? He is my elder brother but was born a woman.' Dhristadyumna then related the tale of Shikandi.

Krishna knew that Shikandi could not win against Bhisma in a one-to-one combat but would make Bhisma lay down his arms since Bhisma would see Amba in Shikandi and he would not fight Amba, the woman. Krishna said, 'Let Shikandi ride in Arjuna's chariot. Bhisma will lay down his arms when he sees her. At that instant Arjuna will shoot arrows and kill Bhisma.'

The tenth day dawned and Krishna drove Shikandi and Arjuna in the chariot towards Bhisma. Seeing them Duryodhana realized their plan and asked all the warriors in his army to create a wall so that Arjuna and Shikandi would not be able to come face-to-face with Bhisma. However, Krishna was a skilled charioteer and brought the chariot in front of Bhisma. Seeing them, Bhisma put his bow down and roared, 'I cannot fight a woman'. Krishna ordered Shikandi and Arjuna to release their arrows. Arjuna protested that it was wrong to shoot an unarmed person. Krishna answered that it was Bhisma himself who chose to keep his weapons down. A volley of arrows were released and Bhisma fell, but not to the ground. Bhisma asked Arjuna to create a bed of arrows for him. Seeing him fall, Drona recalled the troops from the field and fighting was ended for the day. The Kauravas and Pandavas surrounded Bhisma, who spoke to all. Bhisma asked for a pillow for his head and Arjuna immediately shot arrows and placed Bhisma's head on them. Then Bhisma asked for water. Arjuna shot a shaft into the earth and out came Gangaa herself to quench the thirst of her son, Devavrata. Night fell and all of those assembled left one by one. Bhisma once again advised Duryodhana against the foolishness of war and told him to seek forgiveness of the Pandavas. Duryodhana remained silent and Bhisma knew in his heart that his words fell on deaf ears.

When Karna learnt about Bhisma's fall he was stunned and sat for a long time immobilized. Then he aroused himself and went where Bhisma lay. He fell at Bhisma's feet holding them in his hands. He said, 'I, Karna, have come to pay respects to you. I would have come earlier but did not want anyone to see me.' Bhisma said, 'My dear Karna, I know that you are my grandson. Even Vidura knows it. But I have always decried you because you would speak against the Pandavas in support of Duryodhana. I would be happy if you join the Pandavas and end this war.' Karna, however, could not agree as he had vowed to Duryodhana that he would do whatever Duryodhana asked of him. Karna then asked Bhisma to bless him and keep his identity a secret until the war ended, and returned to the tent.

Bhisma lay on a bed of arrows till the last day of war and only after Duryodhana had died, did Bhisma desire his own death and was thus finally released from his mortal body.

Amba's vengeance was fulfilled as in the form of Shikhandi, she became the cause of Bhisma's death.

chapter 2

Drona Meets His End

After the fall of Bhisma, the Kauravas were desperate. They now looked at Karna as their only hope. Karna consoled Duryodhana, and advised him to appoint Drona as the supreme commander of the Kaurava forces. Karna joined the war as Drona did not forbid him from doing so. Drona ably led the Kaurava armies. On the eleventh and twelfth days, at Duryodhana's request, Drona tried his best to capture Yudhisthira alive. The Kauravas thought that with the capture of Yudhisthira, the Pandavas would surrender. In spite of fighting valiantly Drona was unable to capture Yudhisthira as the Pandavas who had learned of Drona's plan from their spies, kept constant guard over Yudhisthira. On the twelfth day, the Kaurava army suffered heavy losses and Duryodhana lost his son Lakshmana. Duryodhana was inconsolable, his fury and sorrow indescribable. When he recovered, he masterminded a plan for the thirteenth day whereby Arjuna and Krishna had to leave the battle to fight the Samasaptakas or Trigarta brothers, who had challenged Arjuna on Duryodhana's instigation. After Arjuna and Krishna left, Drona assembled the army in Chakravyuh formation, or the iron disc of war. Drona was aware that none except Arjuna knew how to enter and exit this strategic formation and hence he chose this when Arjuna was away. However, Abhimanyu, Arjuna's son, had learnt the art of entering the Chakravyuh from Krishna when he was still in his mother Subhadra's womb, having heard Krishna describe it to Subhadra, his sister. But he did not know how to come out from it when overpowered, since Krishna, who was narrating it to Subhadra, had stopped the narrative midway. Bhima promised Abhimanyu that he would follow him like his shadow into the Chakravyuh, and Abhimanyu set off.

Jayadratha had chosen that particular day to invoke Siva's boon of invincibility. So he succeeded in stopping Bhima as the boon gave him the power to stop anyone except Arjuna. Things aligned in such a manner that young Abhimanyu was alone on the battlefield and inside the Chakravyuh, with no guide and no help. He fought valiantly but was slaughtered by the combined assault of several warriors. Karna cut Abhimanyu's bow from behind, Drona killed his horses, Kripa killed his charioteer, the others attacked Abhimanyu with arrows. Finally, when Abhimanyu was faint, Dusshasana's son broke his head with a mace.

At the end of the day, Arjuna returned having vanquished the Samasaptakas only to see the dead body of Abhimanyu. Bhima was inconsolable as he held himself responsible for

Abhimanyu's death. Arjuna realized that Bhima was unable to overpower Jayadratha because Jayadratha had used a boon to protect himself. Arjuna, overcome with grief, vowed that he would kill Jayadratha by sunset the next day or would immolate himself if he failed. This was a terrible oath.

Knowing that Arjuna would immolate himself if he was unable to kill Jayadratha the next day, Jayadratha stayed away. Drona, in order to protect Jayadratha, created a triple vyuha. Drona's plan was that even if Arjuna could penetrate the formations and reach Jayadratha, it would take him a lot of time and the sun would have set by then. As a result Arjuna would not be able to kill Jayadratha, but would give up his own life as he had vowed.

As planned by Drona, Arjuna spent most of the day fighting the various warriors in the different formations who attacked him and kept him busy. Shortly before sunset, Arjuna realized the ploy of the Kauravas and pleaded with Krishna for help. Krishna hid the radiant sun with his discus and it appeared as if the sun had set. Jayadratha came out uncovered. As soon as Jayadratha was spotted, Krishna removed his discus to uncover the sun, and Arjuna cut off Jayadratha's head with an arrow.

Jayadratha's father had granted his son a boon. By that boon, anyone who caused Jayadratha's head to fall on the ground—thereby causing his death—would also die as his own head would shatter into a thousand pieces. Knowing this secret, Krishna adviced Arjuna to shoot his arrow in such a way that it would sever Jayadratha's head and carry it along to deposit it in Jayadratha's father's lap. Jayadratha's father was in meditation at that time and he instinctively stood up—thus dropping his son's head on the earth. Immediately the head of Jayadratha's father split into a thousand pieces and he died.

After four days of fighting with Drona at the helm of the Kaurava army and heavy losses on both sides, the Pandavas met for a discussion. Dhristadyumna reminded them that he was born of the sacrificial fire as a boon to fulfil his father Drupada's only desire—to kill Drona.

Krishna intervened, 'No one can kill Drona as long as he is ready to fight. Drona has to give up his arms. Only at such a time can Dhristadyumna kill him.' Arjuna asked, 'How is this possible?' Krishna said, 'Drona will drop his weapons only if his son dies. Drona will want to go to heaven to question Yamadharmaraja how Aswathama could die, because he knows that Aswathama has been granted eternal life.' Krishna paused and looked at Yudhisthira. 'You must tell Drona that Aswathama is dead. Drona will only believe you.' Hearing this, Yudhisthira's face drained of its colour, 'I cannot tell a lie!' Bhima came to the rescue saying, 'I will kill an elephant called Aswathama. You can then truly tell Drona that Aswathama is dead. But don't mention that it is the elephant and not his son.' Yudhisthira felt that it was not right but he could not see any other way out.

As planned, on the fifteenth day of the war Bhima killed the elephant Aswathama. Then Bhima came to Drona and shouted with glee, 'O Reverend Sir! I have killed Aswathama.

I have killed Aswathama.' Drona couldn't believe his ears. He immediately drove his chariot towards Yudhisthira and asked him if what Bhima was saying was the truth. Yudhisthira said, 'Yes, Aswathama is dead.' Then added in a whisper, 'But it is only an elephant.' Bhima ensured that drums were beaten loud as soon as Yudhisthira spoke the first sentence. As a result, Drona could not hear the second part. Devastated, Drona got down from the chariot, laying his weapons aside. He sat cross-legged on the battle ground and by his yogic power ascended the heavens to question Yama. Taking this opportunity, Dhristadyumna cut off Drona's head.

chapter 3

Curses Come Together for Karna

Karna had not been allowed to participate in the war by Bhisma who considered him a charioteer's son and therefore not fit to fight along his side. Once Drona became the commander, Karna began participating in the war. On the morning of the eleventh day, after performing his morning prayers to the Sun god as was his daily routine, Karna found Kunti, standing there. He saluted her and asked her how he could be of service to her. Kunti was there on Krishna's instructions and said, 'My son, I want you to grant me your solemn vow that you will not kill my sons.' Karna replied, 'Devi Kunti! Please do not address me as your son.'

Kunti then told Karna the secret of his birth and asked him to come over to the side of the Pandavas and become king. Hearing this, Karna said, 'You may have given birth to me but Radha is the only mother I know and acknowledge. I am called Radheya. I have no particular desire for kingship. I cannot forsake Duryodhana and break my vow of friendship.

I have already given away my armour and earrings which were my divine protection, to Indra, who came to me for alms disguised as a Brahmin. Indra has given me a weapon in return which I intend to use against Arjuna. Therefore I will vow that I will not kill any of your sons except Arjuna. This means that you will always remain the mother of five. Either Arjuna or I will live. Both of us cannot live since I have vowed to kill Arjuna. Once the war is over, if I survive, I will come to stay with you and the other Pandavas.'

Though Kunti felt ashamed of her selfishness, she asked for another vow. 'Please also give me your word that you will not use any divine *astra* twice.'

Karna acquiesced to even this request, knowing that he was thereby making his position on the battlefield weaker. Karna had already used the divyastra given to him by Indra to kill Ghatotkacha, Bhima's son from demoness Hidimba. While giving the weapon, Indra had blessed Karna with the boon that the weapon would not miss its target and would destroy whatever was in its way. Karna had planned to kill Arjuna using the divine weapon, but now, bound by his vow to Kunti, he would not be able to use it on Arjuna when the situation so demanded.

On the sixteenth day of war Karna got the opportunity to fight with each of his brothers, but did not kill any of them, bound as he was by his vow to Kunti. Karna defeated Nakula, then Sahadeva, then Bhima and lastly Yudhishtira but each and every time he only disarmed them and then released them.

Bhima sought out Dusshasana and fulfilled his terrible vow made in the court of Hastinapur when Dusshasana had tried to disrobe Draupadi. In the battleground of Kurukshetra man became animal and this terrible oath was fulfilled. Bhima ripped out Dusshasana's heart and drank his blood. He then took some blood in his cupped palms and went to Draupadi and smeared her hair with it. All were horrified at this terrible act of vengeance.

As evening progressed Karna and Arjuna were engaged in battle. Karna used an arrow possessed by the serpent Takshaka who held a grudge against Arjuna for having destroyed his family in Khandavaprastha, and aimed it at Arjuna's forehead. King Salya advised Karna to target Arjuna's heart but Karna refused saying that a hero does not change his aim. Krishna used his divine powers to press down the chariot and it sank into the earth by an inch. As a result Karna missed his aim and his arrow took away Arjuna's coronet. The spirit of Takshaka came to Karna and asked for another chance to take his revenge but Karna refused to use the same incantation twice since he had promised Kunti not to do so.

As sunset drew near, Krishna drove Arjuna's chariot towards marshy land. Karna followed, and the wheel of his chariot got stuck in the slush. Karna asked his charioteer, King Salya, to help him lift the chariot wheel out of the mud. But King Salya refused flatly, saying, 'O son of a charioteer, I agreed to steer your chariot because Duryodhana forced me to. I hate every minute of this. I am here only to handle the horses, not to do a low-caste's bidding.' Karna got down in desperation and tried to move the wheel. He was confident that Arjuna would wait for him to continue the fight as it was against the rules of war to attack an unarmed person. Karna heaved and hauled but the chariot refused to budge—the curse of Bhoomidevi had come into force!

Krishna ordered Arjuna to attack Karna. When Arjuna protested, 'I cannot do so until he is back on the chariot,' Krishna reminded him of how Karna had conspired with Duryodhana when Draupadi was hauled into Hastinapur court, and of how Karna had joined with the rest to attack and kill Abhimanyu. Upon being reminded of his son's death, Arjuna began shooting arrows. Karna immediately aimed his bow and arrow but failed to remember a single incantation since he could not remember anything he had learnt from his guru Parashurama—the curse of Parashurama that all knowledge gained by deceit would leave him at the moment he needed it the most—came into effect.

As Karna struggled to remember, Arjuna's arrows felled him. Even Surya, his father, could not help him in any way because aeons ago, Surya had been cursed for aiding Sahasrakavaci. Krishna came to Karna and reminded him of his earlier birth as Sahasrakavaci. Krishna blessed Karna and Karna joined his hands in prayer to Krishna with his last breath.

And so all the curses came into force together, across space and time, making Karna's death inevitable.

chapter 4

Beginning of the Inevitable

Duryodhana's grief was untold when he learnt that Karna had been killed by Arjuna. On Aswathama's advice Duryodhana requested King Salya to become the commander and lead the Kaurava forces. Before sunset he was killed by Yudhishtra after a long battle.

As soon as Salya fell, panic spread in the Kaurava army. Duryodhana rallied his troops and began fighting, supported by his uncle Shakuni and Uluka, Shakuni's son. All of Duryodhana's brothers were eventually killed by Bhima, leaving Duryodhana as the sole Kaurav. Seeing this, Shakuni intervened with his son Uluka. Sahadeva and Nakula fought them and finally killed both.

With the death of Sakuni, all of Duryodhana's hopes were killed too. By sunset, of the eleven *Akshauhinis* that Duryodhana had started with, not a single soldier was alive. The Kaurava army was now made up of Duryodhana, Kripa, Aswathama and Kritavarma. The Pandavas too had staggering losses. The battlefield was covered with bodies and blood. The stench was awful. The skies were full of thousands of vultures. The devastation was unimaginable. Dhritarashtra and Gandhari were engulfed in grief as Sanjaya gave them detailed descriptions of the battlefield.

chapter 5

Duryodhana's End

On the evening of the seventeenth day, Duryodhana had to abandon his horse that fell down dead. He walked on till he reached the lake Dwaipayana. The cool waters beckoned him. He knew how to stay inside water for a long time. He entered the depths of the water and sat in meditation. The Pandavas, in the meanwhile, were searching for Duryodhana. They did not meet Kripa, Aswathama and Kritavarma. Unable to find Duryodhana anywhere in the battlefield, the Pandavas returned to their camp. However, Kripa, Aswathama and Kritavarma had seen Duryodhana entering the lake from afar. When Dhritarashtra and Gandhari realized that all their sons were dead and Duryodhana was alone, they came to meet him near the lake in the hope of persuading him to seek peace and save his life. But Duryodhana remained adamant.

At the onset of the war, Gandhari had asked Sage Vedavyasa how she could protect her children. He reminded her of her power of chastity and said that her eyes could bestow an invincible shield on whatever it fell upon. Remembering this, Gandhari asked Duryodhana to come out of the water and meet her in the nude. Duryodhana divested himself of his garments and proceeded from the lake to his mother's tent. Krishna, the omniscient, waylaid him and jeered, 'How can a grownup man appear in front of his mother naked? Atleast cover your manhood'. Shamed by Krishna, Duryodhana covered himself till his knees and went into Gandhari's tent. When she heard him come in, Gandhari turned towards him and removed her blindfold. Immediately shining rays from her eyes momentarily bathed Duryodhana in a golden light. His body got the strength of a diamond. Then Gandhari noticed that a part of her son's body was covered, and she wailed, 'My son why did you do this? I had asked you to come completely naked. Now your thighs will remain vulnerable. What have you done? I gave up all my power to save you and you have brought it to naught!'

Duryodhana said that Krishna had advised him against appearing before Gandhari, naked. Gandhari realized what Krishna had done, and in a flash she remembered Bhima's vow—he would break Duryodhana's thighs. In that moment Gandhari understood that it was all over and nothing could save her beloved sole surviving son.

After this meeting, Duryodhana went back to the lake and hid himself there. However, the Pandavas located him and began taunting him for his cowardice. When Duryodhana could no longer bear their goading he came out of the water to face the Pandavas. Yudhisthira gave Duryodhana the option to choose his opponent and the weapon he wanted to fight with saying that if Duryodhana won, then the kingdom of Hastinapur would be his. Duryodhana chose the person he hated the most and a weapon which he loved—Bhima and the mace.

The last match began. Bhima and Duryodhana took up their maces and fought with each other long and hard. Soon Bhima realized that it would be sunset and he would not be able to kill Duryodhana. Due to Gandhari's blessing Duryodhana's body had gained the strength of a diamond and could not be hurt even by the hardest of blows. Bhima sought Krishna with his eyes. Krishna clapped his palm against his thigh. Bhima immediately understood that though hitting the thigh was forbidden, it was the only part of Duryodhana that was vulnerable. Bhima raised his mace and brought it down on Duryodhana's thighs and a terrible sound of breaking bones tore the air. Duryodhana screamed in pain and fell to the ground.

Bhima had finally fulfilled all the vows that he had taken when Dusshasana had attempted to disrobe Draupadi.

The Pandavas left Duryodhana to bleed to death and returned to their tents. The war had finally ended. All the Kauravas were dead and their armies razed to the ground. None of their allies remained. The Pandavas too had suffered severe losses. Only Aswathama, Kritavarma and Kripa lived of those who had fought against the Pandavas as all three had the gift of everlasting life—they were Chiranjeevis. On the Pandavas side, their children through Draupadi, the

Upapandavas, Satyaki, Yuyutsu, Dhristadyumna and Krishna survived.

When Aswathama learnt of Duryodhana's defeat, he came to where Duryodhana was lying in pain and took a vow to destroy the Pandavas. Duryodhana was thrilled to hear his words and asked him to proceed with his mission. Aswathama shared his idea of killing the Pandavas and the Panchalas (Dhristadyumna who had killed Drona unfairly) with Kritavarma and Kripacharya. They tried their best to dissuade him that he would be morally wrong in doing so as the war had ended. When they failed to stop him, they accompanied him to the Pandava camp and there Aswathama slaughtered everyone to death while Kripa and Kritavarma stood on either end to prevent anyone from fleeing. Aswathama took the five heads with him and went to Duryodhana to give him the good news. Duryodhana said, 'Show me Bhima's head'. Aswathama took out the biggest head and gave it to Duryodhana. Duryodhana laughed in derision, 'This is not Bhima's head. This is the son of Bhima. Alas, Aswathama, you have been deceived. You have been unable to keep your vow.' So saying, Duryodhana fell dead.

What had happened was indeed a play of Fate. A few minutes before Aswathama and others reached the encampment of the Pandavas and Panchalas, Krishna had taken the Pandavas outside on the pretext of discussing the future. As a result, the Pandavas had been saved and Krishna had kept his word to Draupadi—'I will ensure that your five husbands live beyond the war.'

When the Pandavas returned and saw the havoc wrought by Aswathama, Kripacharya and Kritavarma, they were plunged in grief. Their fury knew no bounds and they hunted down Aswathama. Aswathama made a final attempt to destroy the race of the Pandavas. He took a blade of grass and chanting the Brahmastra, directed it towards the womb of Uttaraa who was heavy with Abhimanyu's child. In the meantime, the Pandavas reached and Arjuna sent out the same Brahmastra to counter Aswathama's arrow. Krishna asked both Arjuna and Aswathama to take back their missiles, telling them that the entire world would be consumed in the aftermath of these Brahmastras. Arjuna immediately retracted his arrow but Aswathama did not know how to retract the missile. So Krishna placed his discus over Uttaraa's womb, deflecting and reversing the direction of the missile that turned back to Aswathama, asking for its thirst to be quenched. Bhima tore the jewel in his forehead and submitted it to the arrow in order to appease it, leaving Aswathama to bleed constantly. Aswathama was a Chiranjeevi 'immortal' and could not be killed. It is said that even now he roams the forests in the Himalayas, grieving over his sins and bearing the pain of his ever-bleeding wound.

Later, Uttaraa gave birth to a lifeless child but it was brought to life by Krishna. He was called Parikshit.

chapter 6

After the War

The Pandavas approached Dhritarashtra and Gandhari and begged forgiveness for the massacre of their children. Dhritarashtra in his anger and grief attempted to embrace and crush Bhima but Krishna pushed towards Dritarashtra an iron figure instead, which Dhritarashtra crushed into pieces with his bare hands. When Dhritarashtra realized his folly, he broke down in repentance.

Gandhari was so charged with grief that even through her blindfold eyes her emotion seared the foot of Yudhisthira. Gandhari held Krishna responsible for the great war and cursed Krishna that his Yadava race would be destroyed just as her race had been wiped out.

Krishna welcomed her curse since his dynasty was otherwise indestructible, and could only be destroyed by themselves through infighting. Krishna accepted Gandhari's curse with fortitude and assured her that her curse would come true. The main purpose of Krishna's life was to relieve

Goddess Bhoomi Devi—Mother Earth—from the burden of evil-doers.

Once their anger subsided, Krishna appealed to their sense of justice and fairness and requested Dhritarashtra and Gandhari to accept the Pandavas and live with them in peace.

The Pandavas mourned for all the heroes, especially for Karna, who was their own brother and yet had to fight against them. Yudhishtira was advised by Sage Vyasa to take instructions from Bhisma on how to rule the kingdom wisely. The Pandavas approached Bhisma as he lay on the bed of arrows. Bhisma imparted all the knowledge he had obtained from the divine preceptor Brihaspati. He also uttered the thousand names of the Supreme One—the *Vishnu Sahasranaama*. After the teaching was complete, Yudhishtira returned to Hastinapur while Bhisma awaited the coming of Uttarayana, the auspicious time he had chosen to die.

When the holy day came, everyone assembled at Bhisma's feet for the last time. Each person saluted him and took his blessings. Bhisma then called for flowers and worshipped Krishna. He received the blessings of Krishna and willed himself to die, having fulfilled his vow to Satyavati that he would guard the throne of Hastinapur with his life and see that her rightful heir would ascend it.

Yudhisthira was eventually crowned king and Krishna returned to Dwaraka.

All the curses, boons and vows had thus been fulfilled, and all the events had taken shape out of the actions and inactions of the characters involved in this majestic epic.

chapter 7

The End of Dwapara Yuga

Krishna left Hastinapur and returned to Dwaraka after the Great War. Thirty-six years went by. It was time for the curse of Gandhari to be fulfilled. Another curse preceded Gandhari's curse and helped the completion of Gandhari's curse. A boon was fulfilled too.

Once the sages Viswamitra, Kanva and Narada were visiting Dwaraka. Some youngsters played a practical joke on them. They dressed Samba, the son of Jambavati and Krishna, as a pregnant woman, and taking him to the rishis asked their blessings: 'O Great Sages, this woman is expecting a child. Can you please bless the child and tell us if it will be a son or a daughter?'

The sages were enraged at being made fun of by youngsters. They immediately cursed thus: 'This so-called woman will give birth to a mace and that mace will have the power to destroy the entire *Vrishni* race.'

The youngsters were horrified and despite their pleas

for forgiveness, the sages neither changed their curse nor gave a solution to reduce its terrible outcome. The sages left the place and the youngsters were left to face the situation. After nine months, Samba gave birth to an iron mace. The boys went to Krishna and Balarama and told them what had happened. Balarama was upset and ordered that the mace be crushed to powder and the powder thrown into the sea. The order was speedily carried out and everyone forgot the incident of the curse.

But curses will bear themselves out, no matter what happens. One day, the entire family set out for pilgrimage to Prabhasateertha, for the worship of Siva. Only Krishna, being able to foresee the future, knew this was the last trip for all of them. Once they reached Prabhasateertha, tents were pitched and all rested for the night. The next days were spent in games of several kinds. In the midst of merrymaking, one day someone insulted another, and one thing led to another till very soon everyone was fighting. Those who did not have weapons pulled out the weeds and twigs. These were deadly weeds that had sprouted from the powdered mace thrown into the sea several years ago. To their horror, each clump of weed turned into a mace in their hands! The entire group was destroyed in no time. The curse of the mace had come true, and the crushing had only ensured multiple maces—each potent with the power of annihilation.

Everyone died except Krishna, Balarama and Daruka. Krishna sent Daruka to Hastinapur with a message for Arjuna to come to Dwaraka and protect the women and children left there. After Daruka proceeded to Hastinapur, Krishna noticed that Balarama was missing. Krishna went in search of Balarama and saw him leaning against a tree in a deep trance. As Krishna watched, a huge serpent emerged from Balarama's mouth and disappeared into the sea. Balarama, being the incarnation of Sesha Nag, took his real form and left this world.

Krishna then sat under a tree and went to sleep. There was a hunter in the neighbourhood. He saw Krishna's foot and mistaking it to be part of an animal, shot an arrow at it. The hunter was using a piece of iron that he had found by the seashore, and had moulded it into his arrowhead. This bit of iron was actually a piece left behind of the mace born of Samba, that had been ground and thrown into the sea. Hearing Krishna's cry of pain, the hunter came near and was horror-stricken to see that he had killed a man instead of an animal. Krishna with his last breath forgave the hunter, saying it was as ordained, and he was not to blame. The hunter was Vali reborn. Vali's boon was thus fulfilled.

Gandhari's curse had finally come true.

Having received Krishna's message from Daruka, Arjuna took the womenfolk and children along. Once they reached the outskirts of Dwaraka the sea rushed into the city and covered it. Even as they looked, Dwaraka became a memory. On the way to Hastinapur robbers attacked them and carried away everything. Arjuna tried to fight them but found that he could neither use the Gandiva nor remember any incantations. He was totally powerless. He then realized that without Krishna he was nothing. He also realized his earlier self and that it was time to return from this earth to where he actually belonged.

Arjuna related all that had occurred, including how he was unable to use the Gandiva against the robbers. The Pandavas listened in stunned silence. All of them came to the same realization—it was time to leave the earth and set out on their last journey.

Yudhishtira made all necessary arrangements and crowned Parikshit king. Yuyutsu was appointed as his guardian and Kripa as his guru. When Yudhishtira announced their decision, the people tried their best to convince them to stay but to no avail. The Pandavas and Draupadi stood in front of the palace doors clad in tree bark and deerskin. They looked the same as they did years ago, when they were exiled from Hastinapur. But this time they were at peace.

They travelled towards the great Himalayas. They were climbing the mountain Meru when suddenly Draupadi dropped down dead. One after another the Pandavas fell down dead and finally only Yudhishtira and a dog were left. The dog had been following them since they left Hastinapur. Then Yudhishtira saw Indra come with a chariot for him but Yudhishtira refused to go with Indra since Indra asked Yudhishtira to abandon the dog if he wanted to reach heaven and meet his dead brothers. Hearing Yudhishtira's decision, the dog took its real form. It was Dharmaraja who had come for his boon-son!

Yudhishtira was then taken to heaven by Indra but there he found everyone who had died on the battlefield except for his brothers and Draupadi. He was shocked when he saw Duryodhana seated there. He requested Indra to take him to where his brothers were. He was taken to hell and Yudhishtira was surprised that his brothers and Karna were there and not in heaven. He sent away the attendants who had led him to hell with a message to Indra that he preferred to stay in hell with his brothers rather than in heaven.

The whole area was suddenly illuminated and all the gods appeared. They blessed Yudhishtira for his righteousness, loyalty and love for his brothers. When Yudhishtira questioned why his brothers and he were in hell while the Kauravas were in heaven, Dharmaraja explained to him thus: 'The rules of heaven are different from that of earth. Depending on one's *karma* one enjoys the fruit. If one has greater good karma then he suffers the punishments for bad karma first and then goes to heaven to enjoy the fruits of his good karma. Once all karma is suitably rewarded, the soul returns to the earth and it takes a new body. If one had committed greater sin than good, he enjoys heaven first and then faces punishments so that the punishments seem harsher. Now that you have spent time in hell, you will take up your place in heaven. All your brothers and Karna were made to stay in hell for the sins they committed and are now in heaven. Their presence here was an illusion to test you. Once again you proved your righteousness. Since you uttered one lie, you were made to see the sights in hell.

Now you are ready to take your rightful place in heaven.'

Yudhishtira then bathed in the heavenly waters, and went to heaven. Krishna was there in the midst of all gods. Yudhishtira was united with his brothers and other heroes who had fought the great battle.

And thus ends the story of *Jaya*.

Epilogue

The characters of Mahabharata are just as human as any of us. They had their virtues and vices. Yudhisthira was the epitome of Dharma and Duryodhana was the personification of greed and hatred. As Duryodhana says to Krishna once, 'Even when we know some action is wrong, we will perform it, and when some action is right, we will not do it.'

Shantanu, even in that old age, having enjoyed life for many years with the beautiful Gangaa, was not satisfied and married a fisherwoman. That was his mistake and thereby he deprived the rightful heir, Devavrata, from inheriting the throne after him.

Satyavati chose to not tell Shantanu that she already had a son born to her from Parashara. She revealed it only when it becomes necessary to get an heir to the throne. By then Shantanu had passed away. She should have heeded her son's advice and waited for the right time when Vyasa would be agreeable to the wives of Chitrangada and Vichitraveerya. Bhisma was always there to look after the kingdom and he wouldn't have usurped it.

In a similar situation, Kunti should have told Bhisma about Karna and probably he would have accepted it as he had already known about Satyavati. Kunti makes the biggest mistake keeping it a secret until the end. She acts against righteousness by asking Karna for boons on the basis of her motherhood—though she had denied it to Karna throughout his life.

The excessive parental love of Dhritarashtra to his first son made him doubly blind to right action. Despite having the best of advisors, he himself became responsible for his son's doom. Bhisma, Drona, and Vidura were all great and wise men and lived by the *shaastras*. But their compulsions made them unable to persuade the blind king to follow Dharma.

The anger of Amba that should have abated over time, and was misguided, made her suffer much. The anger of Bhima turned him into an animal in the battle—committing one of the most grotesque acts of vengeance.

There were those who would not slip from the path of Dharma even when they had to lose everything. And there were also persons who would do any adharma to achieve what they wrongly desired. Truly, Mahabharata is a microcosm of humankind.

It inevitably brings us to the Hindu view of karma. What we have sowed must be reaped. What we earn as *punya* and *paapa* must be enjoyed either in the same life or in the succeeding ones. There is no escape from it. As ordinary men and women, it is alright to have desires. *Artha* and *Kaama* are not evil by themselves. They must, however, be had through

Dharma (*dharmaad arthashca kaamashca*). But most of us live thus: 'I know righteousness but I am not inclined towards it; and I also know what is wrong but I cannot desist from it. (*jaanaami dharmam na ca me pravrttih; jaanaamy adharmam na ca me nivrttih*). That is what makes us human.

Yudhisthira by his strict adherence to truth throughout his life, has shown us that after all it is only truth that triumphs at the end, not falsehood—*satyam eva jayate naanṛtam*, and virtue, if well observed and upheld in all situations, protects us; it will never desert us—*dharmo raksati raksitah*.

This battle has been going on between good and evil in all ages. It was there in Krita Yuga which is however not documented in any kind of epic. It was there in Treta Yuga, the good being represented by Rama and the evil by Ravana and is documented by Valmiki in Ramayana. It was in Dwapara Yuga, the good being represented by the Pandavas and the evil by the Kauravas and is documented in Mahabharata. It is there in Kali Yuga all around us. It will continue to exist as long as this world continues. In all these battles, it is seen that the good overpowers the evil. If the readers of this book can learn a lesson from the lives of the characters of the Mahabharata and try to improve their conduct for the better, I would consider my efforts worthwhile.

Acknowledgements

My sincere thanks to

My sister, H A Pannaga for her unshakeable faith that I could write;

My brother, A Keshav Bharadwaj who has immensely supported me despite his PhD studies;

Rupa Publications for having set me off on my journey and for ensuring that this reaches the readers;

Elina Majumdar, who has been the guiding star I can't thank enough. No praise can express my admiration for her role in the making of this book;

All the members of Rupa family who have worked silently and steadfastly, and who continue to support my endeavour;

My readers, for reading through a story that has been told so many times before, in the fond hope that the book has been able to give some of the enjoyment that I felt while writing it!